JIM THOMPSON
THE GOLDEN GIZMO

James Myers Thompson was born
in Anadarko, Oklahoma, in 1906.
He wrote twenty-six novels, three
novelizations, numerous articles and
stories, and two screenplays (for Stanley
Kubrick's films *The Killing* and *Paths of
Glory*). Films based on his novels include
Coup de Torchon (*Pop. 1280*), *Série
Noire* (*A Hell of a Woman*), *The
Getaway, The Killer Inside Me, The
Grifters, The Kill-Off*, and *After Dark,
My Sweet*.

ALSO BY JIM THOMPSON,
AVAILABLE FROM
VINTAGE CRIME/
BLACK LIZARD

After Dark, My Sweet
The Alcoholics
Bad Boy
The Criminal
Cropper's Cabin
The Getaway
The Grifters
Heed the Thunder
A Hell of a Woman
The Killer Inside Me
The Nothing Man
Nothing More Than Murder
Now and on Earth
Pop. 1280
Recoil
Roughneck
Savage Night
South of Heaven
A Swell-Looking Babe
Texas by the Tail
The Transgressors
Wild Town

THE GOLDEN GIZMO

JIM THOMPSON

VINTAGE CRIME / BLACK LIZARD
VINTAGE BOOKS • A DIVISION OF RANDOM HOUSE, INC. • NEW YORK

First Vintage Crime / Black Lizard Edition,
June 1998

ISBN 0-375-70032-3

www.randomhouse.com

Book design by Iris Weinstein

Printed in the United States of America
10 9 8 7 6 5 4 3 2 1

THE
GOLDEN
GIZMO

1

It was almost quitting time when Toddy met the man with no chin and the talking dog. Almost three in the afternoon.

House to house gold-buyers cannot work much later than three nor much before nine-thirty in the morning. The old trinkets and jewelry they buy are usually stored away. Few housewives will interrupt their after-breakfast or pre-dinner chores to look them up.

Toddy stopped at the end of the block and gave the house before him a swiftly thorough appraisal. It was the last house in this neighborhood. It stood almost fifty yards back from the street, a shingle and stucco bungalow virtually hidden behind an untended foreground of sedge and cedar trees. Crouched at the end of the weed-impaled driveway was a garage, or, rather, Toddy guessed, one end of a three-car garage. An expensive late-model car was in view, and a highly developed sixth sense told Toddy that the other stalls were similarly occupied.

Hesitating, wanting to quit work for the day, Toddy flipped open the lid of the small wooden box he carried and looked inside.

In the concealed bottom of the box were the indispensables of the gold-buying trade: a set of jeweler's scales and weights, a jeweler's loupe—magnifying eyepiece—a small triangular-faced file and a tiny bottle of one hundred percent pure nitric acid. In the tray on top was a considerable quantity of gold-filled and plated slum, mingled with the day's purchases of actual gold. The latter included almost an ounce of high-karat dental gold—bridges, crowns and fillings—plus an approximate two ounces of jewelry, most of it also of above-average quality.

A man who buys three ounces of gold a day is making very good money . . . if he buys at the "right" prices. And Toddy had bought right. For an investment of twenty-two dollars, he had acquired roughly eighty dollars' worth of gold.

It had been a good day, as good as the average, at least. He was under no financial pressure to work longer. If he knocked off now, just a little early, he could miss that clamoring and hopeless chaos which is Los Angeles during rush hours. He could be back in town inside an hour or less.

Elaine always slept late—of necessity. If he got back to the hotel early enough, he might be there before she started stirring around. Before she had a chance to raise any of that peculiarly hideous hell of which only she was capable.

Toddy lighted a cigarette fretfully, all but decided to begin the long trudge back to the bus stop. Still, if he quit early today, he would do it again. It might become a habit with him, complemented by the equally dangerous habit of starting to work late. Eventually, he would be working no more than an hour a day. And then the day would come when he would not work at all. That would be the end, brother. The end for him and a much quicker and more unpleasant end for Elaine. For regardless of her vain and frequent boasting, no one else but he would put up with her indefinitely.

With a shrug, he ground out the cigarette beneath his heel and took a decisive step up the walk. Swearing silently, he stopped again. Dammit, it was *almost* three— only ten minutes of. And it was such a hell of a gloomy day. Smog had settled over the city like a sponge. Gray, dank, sun-obscuring smog. Even if Elaine was all right when she awakened, the smog would start her off. She'd be depressed and blue, and if he wasn't there . . .

Not only that, but he would be wasting his time at this particular house. Obviously, wealthy people lived here, despite the air of desolation. And wealthy people, even when they were inclined to dispose of their old gold, usually knew its value too well to make the transaction profitable.

"Sharp" gold-buyers have no contact with the law . . . willingly. The law, as they well know, takes a very dim view of their activities. Their licenses may be in order; they may have done nothing provably illegal. Still, a steady stream of complaints flows in their wake, and the police become irritated. The police reason that a man who persuades a housewife to sell him a hundred-dollar watch for five possesses no very high moral tone. He need get out of line very little, rub them the wrong way in the slightest, to be jailed for investigation and eventually "floated" out of town.

Toddy had stayed clear of the police so far, and he intended to keep right on doing so. There'd be no floater for him if he was ever picked up. Once they fingerprinted him, they'd be passing him from city to city until he got train sick. He couldn't remember all the places where he was wanted, but he knew there were a great many.

But—and he hated to admit it, in this instance—he was in little danger from the police unless he deliberately and flagrantly annoyed them. If he had run out of cards, the situation would have been different. But he had not run out; he was always careful to keep supplied. His reluctant fingers found one now, drew it from the breast pocket of his smart tweed coat.

Mr. Toddmore Kent
Special Representative
LOS ANGELES JEWEL & WATCH CO.
Brokers In
Gold Silver Platinum

The Los Angeles Jewel & Watch Co. was a side-street watch-repair shop. Its owner was a beer-loving, bighearted little Dutchman named Milt Vonderheim.

Most wholesale buyers of precious metals give their door-to-door men the same kind of skinning that the latter deal out to their clients. They downgrade your ten-karat gold to eight; they weigh coin and sterling silver together; they "steal" your platinum at a price merely twice as high as that of twenty-four-karat gold. But tubby little Milt, with his beer breath and perpetual smile, was the golden exception to the base rule of other buyers. . . . So a man needed his money every night—was that a reason to rob him blind? So he had no regular residence in the city and was at the mercy of one who did—should you charge him a profit for not speaking to the police?

Milt didn't think so. Milt's prices were only a few cents lower than those of the U.S. Mint, to whom he sold the stuff which Toddy and a number of other young men sold to him. Milt paid five dollars a pennyweight—one twentieth of a troy ounce—for platinum. If you'd have a lean day, he was very apt to upgrade your stuff; pay you fourteen-karat prices, say, for ten.

Nor was that all Milt did: fat, shabby little Milt, edging deeper and deeper into poverty. Milt supplied these cards which were literally worth their weight in gold if a cop stopped you. A cop wouldn't bother you when you showed that card, unless he had to. A transient gold-buyer was one thing. A special representative of a long-established local firm, no matter how small, was something else.

Milt had started Toddy out as a gold-buyer a year ago. He had trained him, stood by him through the perils that beset the trade. He had trained other men, too, Toddy knew, most of those who now sold to him, and he stood by them also. But he did not treat them quite the same as he did Toddy. He was always inviting Toddy back into his shop apartment for a beer or a chat. He was always bragging of him.

"That Toddy," he would boast to the other buyers, "from him you could well take a lesson. Regularity, steadiness, that iss the lesson vot Toddy should give you. While you boys are putting on your pants or drinking coffee, Toddy has already made fife dollars."

Toddy's lean face flushed a little as he remembered those boasts. Resolutely, he brushed a bit of cigarette ash from his whipcord trousers, made a slight adjustment on the collar of his tan sports shirt, and turned his pebbled-leather brogans up the walk to the house.

It was even farther away than it had appeared from the street, and he had an uneasy feeling of being watched from the dark interior behind the rusted screen door. But, hell, what was there to be nervy about? He wasn't giving the police any trouble and they weren't giving him any. And what else was there besides a slammed door or a dog? If he was starting to let things like that bother him, he might as well do a high brody right now. He and Elaine together.

He stepped lightly across the porch, splattered with green segments from the cedars, and raised his hand to knock. He jerked it back, startled.

"Yes?" said a man's sharp-soft voice. "What is it? You are selling something, please?"

The man must have been standing right in the door, hidden by the rusted screen and the shadowed room inside. Toddy blinked his eyes, trying to get the daylight out of them, but he still couldn't see the guy. All he knew about him was his voice—a Spanish-sounding voice.

"Not at all, sir," said Toddy, with energetic joviality. "I'm not selling a thing. A friend of yours suggested that I call on you. If I can give you my card . . ."

The screen opened and a bony, hair-tufted hand emerged. Deftly, it plucked the card from his fingers and disappeared. Toddy shifted uncomfortably.

This was all wrong, he knew. The spiel was off-key here, the gimmick was out of place. He had learned to use the card as a door-opener—to get 'em curious. To force them outside, or to get him in. He had learned to mention a neighbor, or, better still, a "friend." If they fell for it—and why shouldn't some neighbor or friend have suggested a call?—it was all to the good. If they got funny or sharp, he could have the "wrong house," lie out of it some way.

You had to do those things.

Toddy wished that he hadn't done them here.

He looked behind him, down the long inviting walk. He gave a slight hitch to his trousers and snuggled the box firmly under his arm. He'd give some excuse and beat it out of here. Or just beat it without saying anything. After all, he—he—

The screen door swung open, wide.

Through it, with stately but threatening grace, stalked the biggest dog Toddy had ever seen. He did not realize just how big it was until a moment later.

He knew very little about dogs, but he recognized this one as a Doberman. Slowly, it lowered its great pear-shaped head to his feet and examined each in turn. With awful deliberation, the animal sniffed each leg. It looked up at him thoughtfully, appraising him.

Silently, it reared up on its hind legs.

The front paws came down on Toddy's shoulders. The black muzzle almost rested against his nose.

Toddy stared into the beast's eyes. He stared unwinkingly, afraid to move or speak. He stopped breathing and was too fear-stricken to know it.

The screen door closed, slammed at last by its aged spring. As from a great distance, Toddy heard the man's amused chuckle, a seemingly unending chuckle; then, a sharp "Perrito!"—Spanish for "little dog."

The dog's ears pricked to attention. "Ssor-ree," the dog said courteously. "Ssss ssor-ree."

"D-don't m-mention it," Toddy stammered. "A mistake. I m-mean—"

The dog dropped back down to the porch and took up a position behind him. The screen door opened again.

"Please to come in," said the man.

"I don't—that d-dog," said Toddy. *Dammit, was he dreaming this?* "Won't he . . . will he hurt anyone?"

"On the contrary," the man said, and, helplessly, Toddy stepped inside. "He kills quite painlessly."

2

Todd Kent (the *more* was phony) had been born with a gizmo. That—the GI term for the unidentifiable—was the way he had come to think of something that changed in value from day to day, that was too whimsical in its influence to be bracketed as a gift, talent, aptitude or trait.

For most of the thirty years of his life, the gizmo had pushed him into the smelly caverns where the easy money lay. All his life—and always without warning—it had hustled him out through soul-skinning, nerve-searing exits.

A runaway from a broken home, Todd had first hit the big dough when he was sixteen. He had landed as a bellboy in a big hotel. From that he advanced to bell captain, and he was in; the gizmo went to work. Before it was all over the job of bellboy in that hotel was priced at one thousand dollars—a sum which the purchasers grimly went about recovering (along with considerably more!) in various shady ways. Before it was all over—when the beefs flowed over Toddy's young head and those of the minor executives he had fixed—many of the bellboys were in jail and the hotel had a thoroughly bad name.

Toddy was too young to prosecute on a job-selling rap. But there was such a thing as a juvenile authority which could take charge of him until he was twenty-one. Not at all pleased with this prospect, he had a confidential talk with the hotel's lawyers. The result was that he left town . . . but without his spanking new Cadillac, his diamond rings and the contents of his safety deposit box.

In a trackside jungle, he watched an ancient and browbeaten bum toss dice from a rusted can. The bum put the dice in the can, shook them vigorously and threw a point. Then he reshook them, rolled them again, and there was his point. Not immediately—it usually took several throws—and not always. But almost always. Often enough.

Toddy's gizmo swung into action.

Yeah, the flattered bum agreed, it was quite a trick. Any hustler could throw hot dice from his hand, but who'd ever seen it done from a cup? Many big gambling houses insisted on cup shots, particularly where there was heavy money down. They were supposed to be hustler-proof.

No, he'd never got a chance to put the shot to work; stumbled onto it too late for that. But if a guy had the front, the dough, this was how it was done . . .

You held one die on your point. You didn't put it inside the cup. You palmed it and held it outside, pressed against the cup in your shooting hand. Say you were shooting for Phoebe, little five. You held onto three of it, then you rolled, letting the held die spin down at the exact moment the other shot came from the cup. Yeah, sure; maybe fever didn't make. Maybe the free die came out on four and you'd crapped. But you'd lowered the odds against yourself, see, kid? You'd knocked hell out of 'em. And how you could murder them big joints on come and field bets!

Months later . . . but this episode shall be cut short. Months later, in the secluded parlor of a Reno gambling house, a lean taffy-haired young man sat watching a slow-motion picture of himself. The picture had been shot, apparently, from a concealed camera above the crap table, and it showed little but the movements of his hands. But that was enough. That was more than enough. Before the film was half-unwound, Toddy was drawing out his wallet, his bank passbook, and—oh, yes—the keys to a spanking new Cadillac.

He moved into the con games as naturally as a blonde moving into a mink coat. He rode them through Dallas, Houston, Oklahoma City, St. Louis, Omaha, Cleveland, New Orleans, Memphis. . . . He rode them and was ridden, to use a police term. The gizmo was fickle, and he was ridden, rousted and floated.

Since he shunned working with others, he was confined to playing the "small con"—the hype and the smack and the tat. Those, however, with the new twists he added to them, were more than sufficient to provide him with a number of pleasant possessions, not the least of which was a substantial equity in another Cad.

Then, the gizmo becoming frivolous again, it removed these belongings and added his biography (handsomely illustrated) to a volume compiled by the Better Business Bureau. It also left him wanted on seven raps in Chicago, his then base of operations.

That was the gizmo for you. Pushing you into clover one day, booting you into a weedpatch the next.

The gizmo pushed him into the Berlin black market and sixty-three grand in cash. But, naturally, it didn't let him out of the Army with it. What it let him out of the Army with was a six-months' brig tan and a dishonorable discharge.

He wandered out to Los Angeles, hating the gizmo, determined to be rid of it. But the gizmo was stubborn. Wash dishes, drive a cab, peddle brushes?—don't be foolish, Todd*more*. Use your head. You can always see a turn if you look for it. . . . What about all these winos and bums? The town's full of 'em, and they'd sell you their right legs for a buck. They'd sell you their—*blood!* The big labs pay twenty-five a pint for blood. If you did the fronting, sold for fifteen and bought for five . . .

Toddy was in and out of the blood business fast. He

stayed only long enough to get a roll. The scheme was entirely legal. For the first time in his life he was playing something strictly legit . . . and he couldn't take it. If it was legal to nourish the desire to drink with a man's own blood, then he'd go back to his own side of the fence.

He was resting on his roll, deliberating over his next move, when the gizmo shoved Elaine at him. He hadn't had a real roll or even time to take a deep breath since then. He couldn't make enough, no matter what he made, to do the thing that Milt, the gizmo having introduced them, persuaded him he should do. There was good money, legit money, in buying from dentists and other commercial users of gold.

Toddy couldn't have the dough and Elaine, too. Somehow, though he knew Milt was right in so advising him, he couldn't bring himself to boot her out on her tail.

. . . So, now, now the gizmo had led him into this house, into the money *or.* And he had a sneaking hunch that this was going to be something fantastic, even for the gizmo, in the way of *ors.*

3

For the size of the House, the affluence which it outwardly bespoke, it—this living room, at least—was badly, even poorly, furnished. The few chairs, the undersize divan, the table, all were of maple, the cheapest thing on the market. Except for a throw rug or two, the floor was bare.

Toddy looked at the table, where, as a matter of habit, he had placed his open box. He saw now that there was another box on it, a kind of oblong wooden tray. A set of tong-type calipers partly shielded the contents; but despite this and the deep gloom of the room, Toddy could see the outline of a heavy gold watch.

He had taken this in at a glance, his gaze barely wavering from the man. The guy was something to look at. He was the kind of guy you'd automatically keep your eyes on when he was around.

He had no chin. It was as though nose and eyes and a wide thin mouth had been carved out of his neck. Either a thick black wig or a mopline bowl of natural hair topped the neck.

He stared from Toddy to the card, then back again. He waited, a faint look of puzzlement on his white chinless face. He smiled, suddenly, and held the card out to Toddy.

"I can read nothing without my glasses," he smiled, "and, as usual, I seem to have misplaced them. You will explain your business please?"

Toddy retrieved the bit of pasteboard with a twinge of relief. There was something screwy here. It was just as well not to leave his or Milt's name behind him.

"Of course, sir," he said. "I—that dog of yours took my breath away for a moment. I didn't mean to just stand here, taking up your time."

"I am sure of it." The man nodded suavely. "I am certain that you do not mean to do it now. Perhaps, now that you have recovered your breath, Mr.—?

"—Clinton," Toddy lied. "I'm with the California Precious Metals Company. You've probably seen our ads in the papers—world's largest buyers of scrap gold?"

"No. I have seen no such ads."

"That's entirely understandable," Toddy said. "We've discontinued them lately—well, it must have been more than a year ago—in favor of the personal contact method. We—we—"

He stopped talking. He'd seen plenty of pretty girls in his time, many of them in a state which left nothing of their attributes to the imagination. But this . . . this was something else again . . . this girl who had come through the doorway to what was apparently the kitchen. She wore blue Levi's and a worn khaki shirt, and a scuffed pair of sandals encased her feet; and if she had on any make-up Toddy couldn't spot it. And, yet, despite those things, she was out of this world. She was *mmmm-hmmmm* and *wow* and *man-oh-man!*

Toddy stared at her. Eyes narrowing, the man spoke over his shoulder. "Dolores," he said. And as she came forward, he caught her by the bodice and pivoted her in front of Toddy.

"Very nice, eh?" His eyes pointed to her buttocks. "A little full, perhaps, like the breasts, but should one quarrel with bounty? Is not the total effect pleasing? Could one accept less after the warm promise of the mouth, the generous eyes, the sable hair with—"

"Scum," said the girl in almost unaccented English. "Filth," she added tonelessly. "Carrion. Obscenity."

"*¡Vaya!*" the man took a step toward her. "*¡Hija de perro!* I shall teach you manners." He turned back on Toddy, breathing heavily, eyes glinting. "Now, Mr. . . . Mr. Clinton, is it? I have allowed you to study my ward to the fullest. Perhaps you will confine your attention to me for a moment. You said you were sent to me by a friend?"

"Well, I'm not sure she was a friend exactly, but—"

"She?"

"A neighbor of yours. Right down the street here. I—"

"I know none of my neighbors nor are they acquainted with me."

"I—well, it's this way," said Toddy, and his gaze moved nervously from the man to the dog. The big black animal had been lying down. Now he had risen to stand protectively in front of the man, and there was a look about him which Toddy did not like at all.

"I buy gold," said Toddy, flipping open the lid of his box. "I—I—"

"Yes? And just what led you to believe I had any gold to sell?"

"Well, uh, nothing. I mean, a great many people do have and I just assumed that, uh, you might."

The man stared at him unwinkingly, the dog and the man. The silence in the room became unbearable.

"L-look," Toddy stammered. "What's wrong, anyway? Like I say, I'm buying gold—" He picked up the watch on the table. "Old, out-of-date stuff like this—"

That was all he had a chance to say. He was too startled by what followed to realize, or remember, that the watch was ten times heavier than it should have been.

Cursing, the man lurched forward and aimed a kick at Toddy.

Then the dog called Toddy an unpleasant name, the same name the man had called him.

"¡*Cabrone!*" it snapped. *Bastard!*

And then the dog howled insanely and leaped—at the man. For he had received the kick intended for Toddy and in a decidedly tender place.

The watch slid from Toddy's nerveless fingers. He slammed the lid of his box and dashed for the door.

In his last fleeting glimpse of the scene, the dog was stalking the man and the man was kicking and shouting at him. And in the doorway to the kitchen, the girl clutched herself and rocked with hysterical, uncontrollable laughter.

"I," said Toddy, grimly, as he raced toward the Wilshire line bus, "am going to call it a day."

The box seemed unusually heavy, but he thought nothing of it. Late in the day, like this, it had the habit of seeming heavy.

4

Like most people with a tendency to attract trouble, Toddy Kent had a magnificent ability to shake it off. Hot water, figuratively speaking, affected him little more than the literal kind. He forgot it as soon as the moment of burning was past.

This afternoon, then, he was not only troubled and worried but troubled and worried at being so. Sure, he'd had a bad scare, but that had been more than an hour ago. An hour in which he'd ridden into town and had three stiff drinks. Why keep kicking the thing around? What was there to feel blue about? It was even kind of funny when you looked at it the right way.

Irritated and baffled by himself, Toddy turned in at the twelve-foot front of the Los Angeles Jewel & Watch Co.

Most of the shop was in darkness, but the door was unlocked and a light burned at the rear. Milt was reading off a buyer, one of the new ones. And his brogue was as broad as the young man's face was red.

"So! Yet more of it!" Milt slapped aside his brilliant swivel lamp and jerked the jeweler's loupe from his eyes. "Did you look at dis, my brilliant young friend? Did you feel of it, heft it—dis bee-yootiful chunk of eighteen-karat *brass?*"

"Why—why, sure I did, Milt! I—"

"You did not!" the little wholesaler proclaimed with mock sternness. "I refuse to let you so malign yourself! Better I have taught you. Better you would have known. I vill tell you what you felt, my friend, vot you looked at! It was dis bee-yootiful young housewife, was it not? Dot vas where you were feeling and looking!"

A chuckle arose from the other buyers. The young man's voice rose above it.

"But it's stamped, Milt! It's got an eighteen-karat stamp right on it!"

Milt threw up his hands wildly. "Vot have I told you of such? On modern stuff, yess. The karat stamp is good. It means what it says. But the old pieces? Bah! Nodding it means because dere vas no law to make it. It means only dot you must have good eyes. It means only dot you have a file in your box and a vial of acid, and better you should use dem!"

The young man nodded, downcast, and started to move away. Milt beckoned, spoke to him in a harsh stage whisper.

"Tell no vun, but dis time I make it up myself. Next time"—his voice rose to a roar—"FEEL DER GOLD AND NOT DER LADY!"

Everyone laughed, Milt the loudest of all. Then he saw Toddy and hailed him.

"Ah, now here ve have a *real* gold-buyer! What has my Toddy boy brought, heh? Good it will be! Always a good day it is for hot Toddy!"

His voice was a little too hearty, and he stood up as he spoke and jerked his head toward the curtained doorway to his apartment.

"If these gentlemen will excuse us for a moment, I would have a word with you in private."

"Sure," said Toddy. "Sorry to hold you up, boys."

He followed Milt back through the drapes, and the little jeweler whispered to him for a moment. Elaine. Again. He cursed softly and raised his shoulders in a resigned shrug.

"Okay, Milt. I'll come back later and check in."

"You understand, Toddy? There was not much I could do. I could not get away at this hour, for one thing, and the money—I was afraid I would not have so much as was required."

"Forget it," said Toddy. "You've done enough for me without having to take care of her."

Jaw set, he shouldered his way through the drapes again and strode out of the shop. Milt watched him through the door, then sank heavily down into his worn swivel chair. He took a long swig from an opened quart of beer and wiped his mouth distastefully. He looked up into the shrewd-solemn circle of his buyers' faces.

"There," he said, sadly, his dialect forgotten, "is one of the best boys I know. Brains he has, and looks, and deep down inside where it counts, *goodness!* And wasted, all of it is. Thrown away on a—on—"

They nodded. They all knew about Elaine. Toddy didn't talk, of course, except to Milt. And Milt wasn't a gossip either. But they all knew. Elaine got around. Elaine was hot water, circulating under its own power.

"Why don't he dump her, Milt?" It was a buyer named Red. "You can't do anything with a dame like that."

"I have asked myself that," said Milt, absently. "Yes, I have even asked him. And the answer . . . he does not know. Perhaps there is none. The answer is in her, something that cannot be put into words. She is vicious, selfish, totally irresponsible, physically unattractive. And yet there is something . . ."

He spread his hands helplessly.

One by one, the buyers drifted out, but Milt remained at his bench. He was musing, lost in thought. As if it were yesterday he remembered that day a year ago, the first time he had seen Elaine and Toddy Kent.

. . . It had been raining, and Toddy's bare head was wet. He had left Elaine up at the front of the shop and come striding back to the cage by himself.

"I have a watch here," he said, "that belonged to my grandfather. I don't suppose it's worth much intrinsically, but it's very valuable to me as a keepsake. Give it a good going-over, and don't spare any expense. I'll pick it up in a couple of days."

Milt said he would. He would be glad to. He was considerably awed by the young man's manner.

"Oh, yes," said Toddy, and he slapped his pockets. "Just put an extra five dollars on the bill, will you? Or, no, you'd better make it ten. I lost my wallet a little while ago. Think it must have been out in Beverly Hills when I was leaving my bank."

He did it so smoothly that Milt's hand moved automatically toward the cash drawer. Then it stopped, and he looked at the watch and at Toddy, and down the aisle at Elaine.

"It is a disagreeable day," he said. "You and the lady— your wife?—are both wet. If you will step back here, have her step back, I have a small electric heater . . ."

"Some other time," Toddy said, imperiously pleasant. "Just make it ten and—and—"

"Yes," nodded Milt. "My suggestion is good. It is very, very good. Come back, sir, you and your wife."

So they had come back, warily. And Toddy had accepted a brandy in silence. And while he was sipping it, Elaine drank three.

She saw Milt watching her, amazed, and she grinned at him impudently. He looked hastily away.

"Where," he said, "did you lose your wallet?"

"At our hotel." Toddy laughed shortly. "We lost our baggage there, too. And our clothes. Not to mention . . . not to mention anything."

"Ten dollars would do you no good."

"It would get us dinner and breakfast," Toddy shrugged.

"It'd get us into some fleabag for the night. Tomorrow, I'll probably run into something."

"Not tomorrow. You have already run into it. Now."

"Yeah?"

"Yes," nodded Milt. "So I will give you ten dollars and you will visit me tomorrow morning. By tomorrow night, you will have the ten back and twenty, twenty-five, maybe fifty dollars besides."

"Oh, sure," said Toddy. "Sure, I will."

"Surely, you will," said Milt, gravely. "And even if you are not sure, you will be here in the morning. You will be here *because* you are not sure. Is it not so?"

Toddy had looked blank for a moment. Then his eyes narrowed and he grinned. "You've got my number, mister," he said. "I'll be here. And if there's fifty dollars to be made I'll make it."

They had gone out, then, taking Milt's ten dollars with them; and when Milt looked around for the brandy bottle, he found it gone, too.

5

Airedale Aahrens had once broken a man's jaw for asking why he'd been given the handle. It was like asking a one-armed man why he is called Wingie. Airedale had a long thick neck on a short stocky body. His hair was a crisp brownish-yellow, and his eyes were large and liquid and brown.

He didn't speak when Toddy entered the bail bond office. He simply picked up a pencil and the telephone and dialed the police station. After a moment he grunted, "Airedale. What's the score on Mrs. Elaine Kent?"

Toddy drew a chair up to the bondsman's desk and sat down. Elbows on his knees, he studied the familiar abbreviations which Airedale scrawled on a scratchpad:

"DD."

"Drunk and disorderly."

"Assoff."

"Assaulting an officer."

"Rear."

"Resisting arrest."

It was quite a list, even for Elaine. She had obviously been in unusually good form today.

Airedale stopped writing for a moment. Then he wrote "four-bits" and cocked an eye at Toddy. Toddy sighed, made a loop with his thumb and forefinger. Airedale said, "Oke," and slammed up the receiver.

Toddy counted fifty dollars onto the desk, and the bondsman recounted them with thick stubby fingers. He made a balling movement with his hand and the money vanished. He discovered it tucked beneath Toddy's chin, shook his head with enigmatic disapproval, and dropped the bills into a drawer.

Toddy grinned tiredly. He didn't ask why the bond was not put up. He knew it was up. Airedale was in the real estate business. He sold lots. He bought them, too—cheap ones that were plenty adequate for dumps. He'd hold on to them until he needed them, and in the meantime a few hundred bucks slipped to his cousin in the city hall would miraculously produce an official assessment of the land at several times the purchase price—and the value.

Every once in a while somebody would wonder what had happened to all the forfeited bail. Where was the cash? What did the city have to show for it? The cash was in Airedale's pocket, but he'd give the city something to show for it, all right. He was no crook. He'd let the city have a nice thousand-dollar lot for ten or twelve grand in forfeited bail.

Airedale said, "How come they're going after Elaine? They trying to roust you, kid?"

Toddy shrugged. "You know how Elaine is."

"I do," Airedale nodded. "I thought maybe you didn't. You workin' full time as her chump, or can I rent you out? Let me be your agent, kid. They's millions in it."

Toddy chuckled wryly. *Characters,* he thought. *Ten thousand characters and no people.* "Maybe we'd better talk about something else," he suggested.

"Maybe we had," Airedale agreed promptly. "What do you hear from Shake's boys these days? Still trying to chisel in on you?"

"Still trying," Toddy said.

"You don't think they mean business, huh?"

"Probably," Toddy shrugged. "Where they slip up is in not thinking that *we* mean business, too; guys like me. Anyone tough enough to make it in the gold-buying game is plenty tough enough to hold on to what he makes. I'm not going to let a bunch of punks like Shake's tap me for protection. If I scared that easy, I wouldn't be in the racket."

"So? How come Shake's so stupid?"

"He had a little luck. He tapped a few Sunday buyers—old-age pensioners, kids, college boys, people like that."

Airedale nodded appreciatively. He looked toward the door. "Here she comes," he said. "God's little gift to Los Angeles—or why people move to Frisco."

Elaine didn't look bad, for Elaine. She always looked mussed and sloppy and she looked no more than that now. Though she was grinning, a delightful, elfin, heart-warming grin, it was immediately apparent that she had heard Airedale's remark. She made an obscene gesture with her forefinger.

"You can kiss my ass, you fat-mouthed, nosey son-of-a-bitch!"

"You mean that one under your nose? Not me, honey. I'm strictly an under-the-skirts guy—the clean stuff, y'know."

"Why, you dirty bas—"

"Knock it off." Toddy grabbed her by the elbow and dragged her toward the door. "That wasn't very funny, Airedale."

"So who's joking?" said Airedale. He broke into a roar of laughter as they went out, the legs of his chair banging against the floor with the rocking of his body. He stopped at last: wiped his eyes on the sleeve of his checkered shirt. He looked thoughtfully into his cash drawer, then firmly pushed it shut.

Meanwhile, riding toward the hotel in a taxi, Toddy was barely aware of the profane and obscene words which streamed softly, steadily from Elaine's mouth. It wasn't that he was used to such talk; somehow he had never got used to it. In the always-new fascination of watching her face, he simply lost track of what she was saying.

She had perfect control of her expressions. In the space of seconds she could register sorrow, elation, bewilderment, terror, surprise—one after the other. And unless you knew her, and sometimes even when you did, you could not doubt that the pantomimed emotions were anything but genuine.

Her expression now was one of angelic resignation, gentle entreaty. And her words were, "How about it, you stingy bastard? I want a bottle and, by God, I'm gonna get one!"

Toddy shook his head absently, not really hearing her. Her leg slid under his, and the heel of her tiny pump swung back against his crotch. He swore and jerked away. Involuntarily, he swung out and the back of his hand struck her in the face.

It wasn't a hard blow, but it was a noisy one. The cab stopped with a jerk. The driver pushed his hard face over the glass partition.

"What you tryin' to pull, there, Mac?"

"She—" Toddy repressed a groan—"Mind your own business!"

"Like that, huh?" The driver reached for the door. "Maybe I'll make this my business."

"Wait," said Elaine. "Wait, please! It's this way, driver. My husband just got out of jail and his nerves are all on edge—" She let her hands flutter descriptively. "He wanted something to drink, and I didn't want him to have anything. But I guess . . . well, maybe he *does* need it."

"Dammit," snapped Toddy. "I don't want any—"

"Now you know you do, honey." Elaine laid a sympathetic hand on his arm. "He really must, driver. He hardly ever strikes me unless h-he's like this."

The cabbie grunted. "Okay, Mac. You got your own way."

"Give him some money, sweetheart," said Elaine. "You go right ahead and have your whiskey and I won't say a word!"

"I tell you, I'm not—Oh, hell!" said Toddy.

They had stopped in front of a liquor store, of course. Elaine had timed this little frammis right to a *t*. Toddy literally threw a five-dollar bill at the driver. And when the latter returned with a pint of whiskey, he literally threw it and the change at Toddy.

Elaine beamed at both of them. Then she took the bottle with a prettily prim movement and placed it in her outsize purse.

The hotel where Toddy and Elaine lived was a two-hundred-room fleabag a little to the north of Los Angeles' north-south dividing line. Coincidences excepted, its only resemblance to a first-class hotel was its rates.

It was the kind of place where the house dick worked on a commission, and room clerks jumped the counter on tough guys. During the war it had paid for itself several times over by renting rooms to couples who "just wanted to clean up a little." People lived there because they liked such places or because they would not be accepted in better ones.

Toddy's insistence on a second-floor room had immediately identified him to the clerk as a hustler. All the hot guys liked it low down. Down low you could sometimes smell a beef before it hit you. You could sometimes get out ahead of it.

So Toddy had paid an inflated rate to begin with, and, three days later, when his primary reason for wanting a room near the street level became apparent, the rent was boosted another ten a week. The clerk was sympathetic about it, insomuch as he was capable of sympathy. He even declared that Elaine was a mighty sweet little lady. But the rent went up, just the same.

He just had to do it, get me, Kent? The joint's liable, know what I mean? Now, naturally, the best little lady in the world is gonna cut it rough now and then, but people ain't got no sense of humor no more. Toss a jug on 'em from the second floor, an' honest to Christ you'd think they was killed!

Toddy had paid the extra ten without protest, and in return strong iron-wire screens went over the windows. And a hell of a lot of good they did! An empty bottle couldn't be hurled through them, but heavier objects could be— and were. So Toddy rented a room on the alley, the single window of which was protected pretty adequately by the fire escape. Of course, you could get stuff past the fire escape if you tried hard enough.

From the standpoint of comfort, it was by far the worst room Toddy and Elaine had lived in. It was badly ventilated and poorly lit. Even in the coldest days of winter (Oh, yes, it does get cold in California!) it was almost unbearably warm. The virtually uninsulated stack of the hotel's incinerator passed through one corner of the room, and the heat from it was like an oven's. Once, on one of her rampages, Elaine had loosened the clamp which held the square metal column to the wall. And before Toddy could get it back into place, re-join the loosened joints, his face was scarlet from its blast.

He had complained about the thing to the management, not asking its removal, of course, which was impossible, but requesting that its dangerously loose condition be corrected. The management had advised him that if the stack was loose, so was his baggage. There were no nails holding it to the floor, and if he disliked his environment he could move the hell out. The management was getting a bellyful of Toddy and Elaine Kent.

On this particular evening, Toddy followed Elaine down the long frayed red carpet of the hall, past the smells of gin and incense, the sounds of sickness, sex and low revelry. He unlocked the door of their room and stood aside for her to precede him. He closed it, set his gold-buyer's box upon the writing table, and sank into a chair.

Elaine sat half-on half-off the bed, her back to its head. She loosened the foil on the bottle with her teeth, tossed the cap away, and took a long gurgling drink.

"How do you like them apples, prince?" She crinkled her eyes at him. "Prince—spelled with a *k*. What do you say we have another one?"

She had another one and again lowered the bottle. "Well, let's have the sermon, prince. If you don't get started we'll be late for prayer meeting."

"Kid, I—I—" Toddy broke off and rubbed his eyes. "Where do you get the dough to do these things, Elaine! Who gives it to you?"

"Try and find out. Everyone's not as chinchy as you are."

"I'm not stingy. You know that. I'd do anything in the world to help you—really help you."

"Who the hell wants your help?"

"Wherever you get the money, whoever gives it to you, they're not your friends. They're the worst enemies you could have. Can't you see that, kid? Can't you see that some day you're going to get into something that you can't get out of—that neither I nor anyone else can get you out of? You've got intelligence. You—"

He broke off, scowling; for a moment he wanted nothing but to get his hands on her, to—to . . . And then his scowl faded, and the near-murderous impulse passed; and despite himself he chuckled.

Elaine had drawn her face down into a ridiculous mask of solemnity. It was impossible not to laugh at her.

"Okay. So it's no use." He sighed and lighted a cigarette. "Go on and get yourself cleaned up. I'll check in with Milt, and we'll have dinner when I get back."

"Who the hell's dirty? Who wants dinner?"

"You are," said Toddy, rising. "You do. Now, get in that bathroom and get busy!"

Elaine scrambled off the bed and ran to the bathroom door. She paused before it, clutching the knob in one hand, the bottle in the other. Eyes twinkling venomously, she screamed.

The blood-chilling, spine-tingling shrieks piled one upon the other—rose to a crescendo of terror and pain. Then they ended abruptly as she slammed and locked the door.

Above the noise of the shower, he heard her spitefully amused laughter. Trembling a little, he crossed to the phone and waited. It began to ring. He lifted it and spoke dully into the transmitter.

"All right . . . we'll stop. Yeah, yeah. I know. Okay, you don't hear anything now, do you? Well, all right!"

He slammed up the receiver, hesitated glowering. He lighted another cigarette, took a deep consoling puff, and flipped open the lid of his box. He blinked.

What the hell? he thought. *How the hell? Let's see . . . I'd just picked the thing up, and, yeah, the lid of the box was open. And then Chinless tried to kick me, and the dog cut loose, and . . .*

Very slowly his hand dipped down and lifted out the watch . . . the watch from the house of the talking dog.

6

He noticed its weight this time; it sagged in the hand that held it. If he had any ability at all to estimate weights—and he had a great deal—this thing weighed a full pound. Of course, most of that weight would be in the works he knew. Even on the thick old-fashioned jobs like this, the maximum weights on cases seldom ran over thirty pennyweight, one and a half ounces. The case on a modern watch, with its thin movement, would weigh little more than half that much.

He took the loupe from his box and carried the watch over to the dresser. Snapping on a lamp, he made a small scratch in the case with his nail. Loupe in eye, he studied the now-magnified indentation. He whistled softly.

Twenty-four karat. *Twenty-four karat!* The stuff was practically never used in jewelry; never except, perhaps, in insignia and tiny plated areas. It was too soft, not to mention its cost. So . . . ?

Toddy lowered the watch and stood striking it absently against the palm of his hand. There was a tiny *plipping* sound, and the movement, face and crystal flew off. Flew off in one piece. Toddy stared at them, at it—looked from it to the case. He took it in one hand and *it* in the other, and balanced them.

The movement was little larger than a dime. With the things it was affixed to, the crystal and face, it weighed a "weak" five pennyweight. The case, then—the case weighed almost a full pound. There shouldn't be much more than a pound of pure gold in all of Los Angeles County—outside

of government vaults, of course. And yet here was a pound
of the stuff in his hand.

He snapped the two sections of the watch back together,
a tremor of excitement in his fingers, a slow grin lining his
tanned jaw. In a quiet recess of his mind, the gizmo was
awakening. It was kicking back the covers and reaching
under the bed for its bulging kit of angles.

So he'd picked up the watch by accident. So it didn't belong to him. So what? Maybe the chinless guy would like
to claim title to it. Maybe he'd like to explain what he was
doing with—well, call it by its right name—a pound of
twenty-four-karat, .999 fine bullion.

Of course, Chinless didn't look like a guy who'd make
many explanations. He didn't look like a nice guy at all to
tangle with. Still, he wouldn't be stupid enough to raise a
stink over this. Or would he? Toddy wasn't sure—but then
he'd never been a sure-thing player. This was worth gambling on; he was sure of that.

The movement was worthless as a timekeeper. It
wouldn't run more than a few hours before it gave up the
ghost. It served only to disguise the true nature of the
watch. And no one would take such pains, go to such expense, with only one watch. There would be other—yes,
and other items besides watches. Articles that weighed
many times the amount their appearance indicated. If a
man could move in on a setup like that—

Toddy paused in his scheming, listening to the chatter of
the bathroom shower. The light of excitement dulled in his
fine gray eyes. What was the use? What good would it do?
No matter what he made it would all go the same way.
Down the bottomless rat-holes which Elaine burrowed
endlessly.

. . . Box under his arm, he closed the door of the room
and walked down the long hall to the stairs. He went out

through the side entrance of the lobby, reconnoitered its smog-bound environs with a glance as deceptively casual as it was automatic. He strolled up to the corner and stood leaning against a lamppost.

Ostensibly, he was waiting for the traffic signal to change. Actually, he was waiting for the man who had been lurking in the shadows of the entrance, a small man with a sunken chest and a snap-brimmed gray hat that was almost as wide as his shoulders. One of Shake's boys—a shiv artist named Donald.

The man approached. He sidled up to the opposite side of the post and spoke from the corner of his mouth.

"Let's have it, Kent. Shake ain't waitin' no longer."

"Cow's ass?" said Toddy, with the inflection of "How's that?"

"I'm not tellin' you again. The next time I see you, you'll have your balls in that box instead of gold."

"Why, Donald!" said Toddy. "How would I close the lid?"

Donald didn't answer him. Donald couldn't. Toddy's arm had curled around the post, around his head, and his nose was flat and getting flatter against the rusty iron. He mumbled, *"Awwf-guho,"* and managed to free the thin steel knife from its hip sheath. Toddy's arm tightened, and he dropped the knife into the gutter.

"Now," said Toddy, "get this clear, once and for all. I'm not paying any protection—not one goddam penny. Don't try for it again. If you do . . . well, just don't."

He released the little shiv artist with a contemptuous twirl. He crossed the street and vanished into the darkness without looking back.

Milt's shop was dark, of course, but the door was unlocked. For a man in the gold racket, Milt's faith in human nature was astonishing.

Toddy made his way down the dark aisle with practiced ease, pushed through the wicket which adjoined the jeweler's cage, and shoved aside the drapes. Milt wasn't in the living room, but an excited clamor from the kitchen told Toddy where he was. Toddy set his box upon the old-fashioned library table, and went on back to the rear room.

As usual, the swarthy and sullen Italian who delivered Milt's beer was late, and, as usual, Milt was reading him off. He followed the man to the back door, gesticulating, complaining with humorous querulousness.

"Have you no sense of the importance of things? Is there no way I can appeal to you? Suppose I had run out! What then, loafer? That means nothing to you, eh, that I should be left here without so much as a swallow—"

The roar of the delivery truck shut off his protest. Muttering, face pink with outrage, he faced Toddy.

"I ask you, my friend, what should I do with such a dummox? What would you do in my case?"

"Just what you do," Toddy chuckled. "You wouldn't know what to do if you didn't have that guy to fight with every night. Anyway, I'll bet you've got your refrigerator full of beer."

"But the principle involved! The fact that I exercise a certain foresight does not affect the principle."

"Okay," said Toddy. "I think I'll drink a bottle of this warm, if you don't mind. On a night like this, I—"

"*Stop!*"

"Huh!" Toddy jerked his hand away from the beer case.

"Never!" said Milt with mock severity. "Never in my house will such a sacrilege be permitted. Warm beer? Ugh! Aside from the shock to the senses, there is no telling what the physical results might be."

"But I like—"

"I will do nothing to nourish such an unnatural appetite. Come! I will get us some that is only mildly cold."

Milt took two bottles from the bottom of the overflowing refrigerator and carried them into the living room. They took chairs on opposite sides of the table, toasted each other silently, and then went to work at grading and weighing the gold.

This, checking-in time, was virtually the only time of day when the scales were in use. Simply by hefting it, any good gold-buyer can tell what an article weighs within a margin of a few grains. His clients can't, of course. They have only the vaguest idea as to the weight of the things they sell. They live in a world of ounces and pounds . . . and they remain there, if the buyer has his way. He won't use his scales unless he has to.

In dealing with Milt, a wholesale buyer, the scales were, naturally, necessary. Estimated weights, correct within a few grains, were not good enough. A grain is only one-four-hundred-and eighth of a troy ounce, but multiplied by several dozen purchases it might cost the wholesaler his week's profit. As for the grading, that went swiftly. The quality of gold is determined by its brightness, and it was seldom that either Milt or Toddy lingered over an article.

Toddy took the bills which Milt gave him, and stuffed them into his wallet. A good day, yes, but if he could turn that watch, that pound of twenty-four-karat bullion now hidden in the back of his dresser drawer. . . . If there was some way of tapping the source of that watch—

"There is," said Milt, "something troubling you, my friend?"

"Oh no." Toddy shook his head. "Just daydreaming. Tell me something, will you, Milt?"

"If I can, yes."

"Where would—how much scrap gold like this would it take to make a pound of twenty-four karat?"

"Well," Milt hesitated. "Your question is a little vague. Scrap of what quality—ten, fourteen, eighteen karat? Say it was all fourteen, well, that is easily estimated. Fourteen karat is sixty per cent pure. Roughly, it would take not quite two pounds of fourteen to refine into one pound of twenty-four."

Toddy whistled. "Where would you get that much gold, Milt?"

"I would not. So much gold, why it is more than two or three of my boys would take in in a week. And if I did buy it, I would not refine it into twenty-four. Why should I? It would gain me nothing. The mint would pay me no more for a pound of twenty-four karat than it would for two pounds, or whatever the exact figure is, of fourteen."

"Suppose you didn't sell it to the mint?"

"But where else would I . . . ohh," said Milt.

"Now, wait a minute—" Toddy held up a hand, grinning. "Don't leap all over me yet. I'm just thinking out loud."

"Such thoughts I do not like."

"But, look, Milt . . . why couldn't a guy do this? Pure gold is staked at thirty-five dollars an ounce in this country. Abroad, it's selling for anywhere from seventy-five to a hundred and fifty—depending on how shaky a nation's currency is. So why couldn't you refine scrap into twenty-four, have it made up into jewelry, trick stuff, you know . . ."

"Yes," said Milt. "I see exactly what you are driving at. The jewelry could be worn into Mexico—for a few dollars; for a task so safe, wearers could be readily secured.

And from Mexico, there would be little difficulty in getting the gold abroad. Yes, I know. I see."

"Well?"

"It is not well and you know it. There are severe penalties for removing gold from this country. Even to be in possession of bullion is a federal offense."

"But the profit, Milt! My God, think—"

"Yes," said Milt sternly. "The profit. My God. My God, is right. How many such profitable enterprises have you undertaken in the past? What was your profit from them? Heh? Shall I refresh your memory, my oh-so-foolish Toddy?"

"Oh, now," said Toddy, coloring a little. "There's no need to bring those things up. Anyway, this is an entirely different deal."

"Now you have your feelings hurt," Milt nodded. "You have given me your confidence and now I remind you of things you would rather forget. Good. I shall continue to hurt your feelings. I shall continue to remind you of the unpleasant conclusions of your past escapades. Better to do that than see you repeat your errors."

"But—" Toddy caught himself. "Oh, well," he said, "what are we arguing about? I told you I was just thinking out loud."

"And I told you it was not good to entertain such thoughts. Why should you dwell on them? At not too great a risk, you are making very good money. You are not known to the police here. Without some deliberate bit of foolishness, you are assured of an excellent income and, more important, your freedom. If, on the other hand, you—"

"I know," said Toddy, a trifle impatiently.

"You do not know. You place too great a store by the

fact that you have not been fingerprinted by the police of this, the City of Angels. You are forgetting the brief but telling physical description of you which is on file at the license bureau. You are forgetting the bureau's reason for having such data—the fact that gold-buyers are always suspect, that it may be necessary to lay hands on them at a moment's notice. You see? You are safe only as long as you commit no overt act. Once you do, the fingerprinting and the discovery of your record will follow as a matter of course."

Toddy took a long slow drink of his beer. "Yeah," he said slowly. "I know. . . . But tell me one thing, Milt, just to satisfy my curiosity. Then I'll shut up."

"If I must."

Say that you did—I know you don't—say that you did want to buy enough scrap of all kinds every week to refine into six or eight pounds of twenty-four karat. Enough to take care of the kind of overhead you'd be bound to have and still make enough of a killing to pay you for the risk. How would you go about it?"

"For me, it would be impossible, as I told you. Some of the larger refineries might buy that much gold."

"But they're checked, aren't they? If their shipments to the mint started falling off—"

"They are checked, yes. There is a check even on such relatively unimportant wholesale buyers as I."

"Huh," Toddy frowned. "How about this, then? Why couldn't you spread your buying through a group of wholesalers—take a pound or less of scrap from each one?"

"Because you could not pay them enough for the risk they were taking. And the secret of your enterprise would be dangerously spread with your buying. . . . So, there is my answer, Toddy. It is an impossibility. It cannot be done."

"But it—I mean—"

"Yes?" said Milt.

"Nothing. Okay, I'm convinced," Toddy grinned. "How about another beer?"

Uncomfortably conscious of Milt's curious and troubled gaze, Toddy left shortly after he had finished the beer. But he was by no means free of the tantalizing reflections which the watch had inspired. They expanded and multiplied in his mind as he strode back through the hazy streets.

Dammit, that gold *was* being bought, regardless of what Milt said. And this *was* entirely different from anything he had ever touched. He'd have to be careful, certainly. He'd have to do some tall scheming. But just because he'd had a few bad breaks in the past, there wasn't any reason to—

Toddy was almost running when he reached the hotel. He ignored the elevator and raced up the steps. He went swiftly down the hall. He shouldn't have left Elaine alone. He shouldn't have left the watch in the room.

His hand trembled on the doorknob. He turned it and went in. The room was dark. He found the light switch and turned it on.

She lay sprawled backwards on the bed. Naked. Sheets tumbled with her strugglings, damp from her bath. Eyes glazed and bloodshot; pushing whitely, enormously from the contorted face. Veins empurpled and distended.

One of the stockings was tied around her throat, knotted and reknotted there, and her stiffening fingers still clawed at it. The other stocking had been stuffed into her mouth; the toe of it, chewed, wet from gagging, edged out through the open froth-covered oval of her lips.

Toddy swayed. *How could I know . . . something I read . . . she was always asking for trouble . . .* He closed his eyes and opened them again. He put a hand out toward her—toward that hideously soggy fragment of stocking. Hastily he jerked the hand back.

The room had been ransacked, of course. Every drawer in the dresser had been jerked out and dumped upon the floor. Toddy's eyes moved from the disarray to the window. He went to it and flung up the shade.

There was a man down there near the foot of the fire escape. He was a small man with a hat almost as wide as his shoulders. One of his feet had slipped through the steps, and he was struggling frantically to free it.

7

Toddy had been sitting on his roll when he met Elaine Ives. He'd built up his wardrobe, had several grand in his kick, and was driving a Cadillac—rented, alas—while he tried to hit upon a line.

Toddy liked nice things. He liked to live in good places. He found that it paid off. In the swank apartment hotel where he resided, he was believed to be the scion of a Texas oil millionaire. No one would have thought of associating the tanned, exquisitely tailored young man with anything off-color.

He was sitting in the bar of his hotel the day he met Elaine. Apparently she had followed him in from the street, although he had not seen her. The first he saw of her was when she slid onto the stool next to his and looked up at him with that funny, open-toothed smile.

"Order yet, darling?" she said. "I believe I'll have a double rye, water on the side."

He looked at the bartender, who was giving Elaine a doubtful but chilly eye. "That sounds good enough for me," he said. "Two double ryes, water on the side."

In the few seemingly casual glances he gave her, while she drank that drink and three others, he checked off her points and added them up to zero. She was scrawny. Her clothes, except for her hat—she was always careful with her hats—looked like they had been thrown on her. The wide-spaced teeth gave her mouth an almost ugly look. When she crinkled her face as she did incessantly, talking, laughing, smiling, she looked astonishingly like a monkey.

Yet, dammit, *and yet* there was something about her

that got him. Something warm and golden that reached out and enveloped him, and drew him closer and closer, yet never close enough. Something that even infected the bartender, making him solicitous with napkins and ice and matches held for cigarettes—that held him there wanting to do things that were paid for by the doing.

Toddy glanced at his watch and slid off the stool. "Getting late," he remarked. "Think we'd better be getting on to dinner, don't you?"

"No," said Elaine promptly, crinkling her face at him. "Not hungry. Gonna stay right here. Jus' me an' you an' nice bartender."

The bartender beamed foolishly and frowned at Toddy. Toddy gave him an appraising stare.

"I think," he said, "the nice bartender is in danger of losing his nice license. Which is worth a nice twenty-five thousand for a nice place like this. It isn't considered nice, it seems, to provide liquor to obviously intoxicated people."

"Not 'tox-toxshi-conshtipated! Ver' reg'lar—"

But now the bartender had become even more urgent than Toddy. And Elaine was holding herself in a little; she wasn't ready to open all the stops. Toddy got her out of there and into the Cadillac, and she passed out immediately.

He opened her purse, looking for something that would give him her address. Its sole contents, aside from compact and lipstick, was a wadded-up letter. He read it with a growing feeling of gladness.

Of course, he'd been sure from the beginning that she wasn't peddling, another b-girl, but he was glad to see the letter nonetheless. Any girl might blow her top if something like this happened to her—having a studio contract canceled before she ever started to work. Hell, he might have gone out hitting up strangers himself. Now, with the letter in his hand, he saw why he had felt that he had known her.

He had seen her several years before in a picture. It had been a lousy picture, but one player—a harried, scatter-witted clerk in a dime store—had almost saved it. She had only to fan the straggling hair from her eyes or hitch the skirt about her scrawny hips to set the audience to howling. They roared with laughter—laughter that was with her, not at her. Laughter with tears in it.

Toddy drove her around until she awakened, and then he drove to a drive-in and fed her tomato soup and coffee. She took these attentions matter-of-factly, trustingly, either not wanting to ask questions or not needing to. He took her to her home, a court apartment in North Hollywood.

He went in with her, steered her through the disarray of dropped clothes and empty bottles and overturned ash-trays to a daybed. She collapsed on it, and was instantly asleep again.

Toddy stared at her, perplexed, wondering what to do, feeling a strange obligation to take care of her. The court door opened unceremoniously and a woman stepped in.

She had a bust on her like a cemetery angel and her face looked just about as stony. But even she looked at Elaine and spoke with a note of regret.

So this was Mr. Ives—the brother Elaine had insisted would arrive. And just when she was beginning to believe there wasn't any brother! Well. She knew how perturbed he must be, she was fond of Elaine herself, and—and such a great talent, Mr. Ives! But it just couldn't go on any longer. She simply could not put up with it. So if Mr. Ives would find her another place immediately, absolutely no later than tomorrow—And since he'd want to get started early, the back rent—six weeks, it was . . .

Toddy paid it. He stayed the night there, sprawled out on two chairs. In the morning, he helped Elaine pack. Or, rather, he packed, stopping frequently to hold her over the toilet while she retched, and washing her face afterward.

He found and paid for another apartment. He put her to bed. Not until then, when she was looking up at him from the pillows—a bottle of whiskey on the reading stand, just as "medicine"—did she seem to take any note of what he had done.

"Sit down here," she said, patting the bed. And he sat down. "And maybe you'd better hold my hand," she said. And he held it. "Now," she said, her face crinkling into a frown, "what am I going to do about you?"

"Do?" Toddy grinned.

"Now, you know what I mean," she said severely. "I'm broke. I'm not working and I don't know when I will be. I guess I should ask you to sleep with me, but I've never done anything like that, and anyway it probably wouldn't be much fun for you, would it? I mean I'm so skinny I'd probably stick you with a bone."

"Y-yes," nodded Toddy. He had the goddamnedest feeling that he was going to bawl!

"Maybe I could wash some clothes for you," said Elaine. "That's an awfully pretty suit you have on. I could wash it real nice for you and hang it out the window, and it . . . would that be worth fifty cents?"

Toddy shook his head. He couldn't speak.

"Well"—her voice was humble—"a quarter, then?"

"D-don't," said Toddy. "Oh, for Christ's sake . . ."

Toddy hadn't cried since the night he ran away from home. He'd half-killed his stepfather with a two-by-four, bashed him over the head as he came into the barn. He'd tried to make it look like an accident, like one of the rafters had broken. But he was shaking with fear, with that and the bitter coldness of the night. He'd huddled down in a corner of the boxcar, and sometime during the night a tramp had crawled into the car also. Observing the proprieties of the road, the tramp had gone into a corner, that corner, to relieve himself. And Toddy had been soaked, along with his thin parcel of sandwiches. The stuff had frozen on him. He'd cried then, for the last time.

Up to now.

He was down on his knees at the side of the bed, and her arms clutched him in an awkward, foolishly sweet embrace, and she was talking to him like a child, as one child to another, and there had never been another moment like this in the history of man and woman. They cried together, two lost children who found comfort and warmth in each other. And then they started to laugh. For somehow in the extravagant and puppyish outpouring of her caresses, she had hooked the armhole of her nightgown around his neck.

While she shrilled gleefully that he was tickling her, and while her small breast pounded his face with merriment, he lifted and stood her on the bed. Then, since there was no other way, he slid off the other shoulder strap and drew the gown off her body, lowering his head with it.

He shucked out of it and turned around. She was still standing upright, examining herself in the wall mirror.

She twisted her neck and gazed at her childish buttocks. She faced the mirror and bowed her back and legs. She raised one leg in the air and looked.

She turned around, frowning, and nodded to him. "Feel . . . no, here, honey. That's where you do it, isn't it?"

Toddy felt.

"Not bad," he said gravely. "Not bad at all."

"Not too skinny?"

"By no means."

Elaine beamed and put her legs back together. Pivoting, arms stiff at her sides, she did a pratfall on the bed. When she stopped bouncing, she lay back and looked at him.

"Well," she said, puzzledly. "I mean, after all . . . hadn't we better get started?"

Thus, the story of the meeting of Toddy and Elaine. Funny-sad, bitter-sweet. It put a lump in your throat; at least, it put one in the throat of Toddy, who lived it. Then, they flew to Yuma that night and were married. And the lump moved up from his throat to his head.

Literally.

They were in their hotel room, and Elaine was teasing for just one "lul old bottle, just a lul one, honey." All her charm was turned on. She pantomimed her tremendous thirst, staggered about the room hand shielding her eyes, a desert wanderer in search of an oasis. Then, she broke into an insanely funny dance of joy as the oasis was discovered—right there on the dresser in the form of his wallet.

Laughing tenderly, Toddy moved in front of her. "Huh-uh, baby. No more tonight."

Elaine picked up the empty bottle and hit him over the head with it. "You stupid son-of-a-bitch," she said, "how long you think I can keep up this clowning?"

8

S hake's headquarters were in a walk-up dump on South Main, a buggy, tottering firetrap tenanted by diseases-of-men doctors, a massage parlor ("cheerful lady attendants") and companies with uniformly small offices and big names. The sign on his smudged windows read, "Easiest Loans in Town." It was true in the same sense, say, that death solves all problems is true.

Without co-signers, collateral or even a job, in the usual meaning of the word, you could borrow from one to a maximum of ten dollars from Shake; and you could—and usually did—take the rest of your lifetime to pay it back. Shake liked to get along with people; he liked to live and let live. He said so himself.

If you objected to these lenient arrangements, things were still made easy for you; there was a swift and simple alternative. Shake's *pachucos,* his young Mexican toughs, would pay you a visit. They would drop around to your one-chair barber shop or your shoeshine stand or the corner where you hustled papers and kick the holy hell out of you. They'd lay you so flat you could crawl under doors. Shake pointed to the expense of these kickings as justification for his whimsical methods of compounding interest.

When Toddy pushed Donald into the office ahead of him, Shake and two of the *pachucos* were in the back room. They'd been splitting a half-gallon of four-bit wine while they stamped phony serial numbers into an equally phony batch of Irish sweepstakes tickets. Their minds were a little muggy and they were jammed around a littered table. Before they could snap together, Toddy had dutch-walked Donald inside and kicked the door shut.

They got to their feet then; they advanced a step in a three-cornered half-circle. But Toddy jerked his head toward the windows and the movement stopped abruptly.

"Come on," he invited grimly. "I won't do a damn thing but toss this bastard out on his skull."

"N-now, T-Toddy . . ." Nervous phlegm burbled in Shake's throat. "Now, Toddy," he whined, "is this a way to act? Bustin' into a office after business hours?"

He was a swollen dropsical giant with an ague, probably syphilis-inspired, which kept his puffed flesh in faint, almost constant oscillation.

"I've got something to say," said Toddy. "If you don't want those punks to hear it, you'd better send 'em out."

"Well, now—" Shake made a flabbily deprecating motion. "I don't know about that. We're settin' here having a nice little party, Ramon an' Juan an' me. Just settin' here minding our own business, and then you come along an'—"

"All right," said Toddy. "I gave you a chance. I went up to my room tonight and—"

"*Wait!* Send 'em out, Shake!"

"Oh?" Shake looked doubtfully at the little shiv artist. "You been up to somethin' bad, Donald?"

"Send 'em out!" Donald gasped, teetering painfully in Toddy's grip. "Do like he says, Shake!"

"Well . . . how far you want 'em to go, Toddy?"

"How good can they hear?"

Shake hesitated, then waved his hand. "All the way down, boys. Clear down in front."

The *pachucos* left, duck-tail haircuts gleaming, heel-plates clicking on the ancient marble. When Toddy heard the outer door close, he released Donald with a shove.

"All right, strip."

"Goddammit, I done tole you I—"

"Take 'em off, Donald." Shake's pig eyes gleamed with interest as he sank into a chair.

Sullenly, Donald shed his clothes until he stood naked before them.

"You're awful dirty, Donald." Shake clucked his tongue reproachfully. "He have a chance to ditch it anywheres, Toddy? Could he of tossed it away?"

"No," Toddy admitted, "he couldn't."

"How big was it? . . . Donald, maybe you better bend over an'—"

Toddy chuckled unwillingly and Donald spewed out outraged obscenities.

"All right, then!" Shake said. "You just get them clothes back on before you catch cold. And, Toddy, maybe you better . . ."

Toddy nodded slowly. "Here it is," he began. "Donald hit me up for protection again tonight, and I gave him a brush-off. One that he'd remember. Then—"

"But that was just business, Toddy! Just because a man's ambitious and wants to expand, it don't prove—"

"It proves you're stupid enough to try anything. Jesus—" Toddy shook his head in wondering disgust. "Trying to shake down a gold-buyer! A bunch of cheap hoods like you. Why the hell don't you work out on Mickey Cohen?"

Shake looked embarrassed. "Well, now," he mumbled. "Maybe it wasn't real smart, but—"

"Smart!" snarled Donald. "You see what the son-of-a-bitch done to my nose?"

"I met Donald on the way to Milt's shop. I went on down to the shop and checked in, then I went back to my room. I couldn't have been gone more than thirty or thirty-five minutes at the outside. When I went in I found the room turned upside down, I found Donald heading

down the fire escape, and I found my wife on the bed . . .
strangled with her own stockings."

"Sss-strangled? . . . Y-you mean h-he . . . ?"

"I didn't!" Donald snapped, fearfully. "Dammit, Shake,
why for would I do a thing like that?"

"W-why for was you in Toddy's room?"

"I—well, I—"

"Spill it!"

Donald edged toward the corner of the room, keeping a
cautious eye on Toddy. "I j-just went up there to wait for
him. Kind of surprise him, you know."

"Yeah?"

"I was—I was just goin' to cut him up a little when he
came back."

Shake sighed with relief. "You see, Toddy? Donald
wouldn't of killed her. Donald ain't that kind of boy. He
was just goin' to cut you up a little."

"Uh-huh. And Elaine jumps him, so he gives her the
business."

"You're a goddam liar!"

"Now you know better than that, Toddy," said Shake.
"You been around too long to think a thing like that. In
the first place, he ain't a killer. In the second place, he's a
shiv man. Why for would he screw around with stockings
when he had a shiv? It ain't his—his—"

—*modus operandi*, Toddy supplied silently. It was true;
the operation method of a criminal almost never changes.
The police would have a hell of a time if it did. Still, Donald had had the opportunity. He'd been caught at the scene
of the murder.

"You think I'm—I'm immortal or somethin?" Donald
demanded with genuine indignation. "You think I'm a
pervert? You think I killed the Black Dahlia?"

"I think you're a very sweet little boy," said Toddy.

"The whole trouble is, people just don't understand you. Like me, for example. How'd you know it was safe to go into my room? How'd you know my wife wasn't in there . . . alive?"

"I could look under the door an' see it was dark. I knocked an' didn't get no answer, so I went in."

"The door was unlocked?"

"I'm tellin' ya."

"How long was this after you left me?"

"Well . . . fifteen-twenty minutes maybe."

"Just long enough to work your nerve up, huh? How long had you been there when I came in? It couldn't have been much more than ten minutes."

"It wasn't." Donald scowled peevishly. "Look. Why don't you cut out the third degree an' let me tell you."

"Okay. Keep it straight."

"I knocked on the door," said Donald. "I knocked an' waited a minute. I thought I heard someone movin' around—kind of a rustlin' sound—and I almost took a powder. But I didn't hear it no more, then, after the first time, so I figured it must be the window shade flappin' or something like that. I opened the door just a crack an' slid in . . ."

"Go on."

"I"—Donald wiped sweat from his face—"I stood there by the door, hugging the wall and waiting . . . an' . . . an' I don't know. I begin to get kind of a funny feeling, like someone was staring at the back of my neck. Well, you know how it is in that room. You can't really see into it up there by the door. You can't see the bed or nothing hardly until you get past the bathroom. Not with the lights off, anyways . . ."

"I know that," said Toddy impatiently.

"Well, I got this feeling so . . . so I slide down along the wall until I'm out of that little areaway. I came even with the bed and my eyes are gettin' kind of used to the dark an' I can see. A little. I can see they's someone on the bed. I— I—Jesus! I can't even think what I'm doin'! All I can think of is lightin' a cigarette—I mean, I don't really think of it. I do it without thinkin'. And then the match flares up an' I see everything. I see what's happened. An' then I hear you at the door, an' I try to beat it down the fire escape an'—"

Toddy nodded absently. Donald was in the clear. He'd been pretty sure right from the beginning. But under the circumstances, there'd been nothing to do but grab him.

Donald stepped to the table, poured out a water glass of sherry, and killed it at a gulp. Shake stroked his chins and stared interestedly at Toddy.

"If you was so sure Donald killed your wife," he said, "why didn't you just call the cops? That's what cops is for, to arrest criminals."

"So that's it," said Toddy. "I often wondered."

"You know what I think?"

"Yes."

"I think you killed her yourself. You either bumped her off before you left the room or—"

"—Or I went up the fire escape and did it, then beat it down and came up the front way." Toddy's tone was light, satirical, but there was a heavy feeling around his heart. Something seemed to struggle there, to fight up toward the hidden recesses of his mind. "Sure. That's what the cops will think. That's what *I'll* say after they work me over a few days."

Shake shook his head with a complete lack of sympathy. "They sure swing a mean hose in this town. You wouldn't believe what it does to a man's kidneys. I had a *pachuco* workin' for me; you remember him, Donald—Pedro? You remember how he went around after the cops had him? All bent together like a horseshoe. Had to take off his collar to pee."

"Think of that," said Toddy.

"Me an' Donald has got a duty to do, Toddy. The only thing is, how long should we take to do it? Now if we was real busy—say, we had some money to count—"

"Huh-uh."

"Huh-uh?"

"In spades."

"Too bad." Shake stared at the telephone. "That certainly is too bad, ain't it, Donald?"

"Oh, it's not too bad yet," said Toddy. "Let's see, now. It would take your *pachucos* a couple of minutes to get up here. That's not much, but I don't think you and Donald can take much. I really don't think you can, Shake. Of course, if you'd like to find out . . ."

He spread his hands, beaming at them mirthlessly. Shake drew the back of his hands across his mouth.

"So you'll sit here the rest of your life?" he burbled.

"All right," said Toddy. "Say that I walk out of here and you use the phone. I know every big-time con man in the country, and con men stick together. I'd make bond eventually. I'd be around to see you. You wouldn't enjoy that, Shake. I tell you from the bottom of my heart you wouldn't."

He stared at them a moment longer, white teeth bared, eyes gray and cold. Then he broke the tension with an easy, good-natured laugh.

"Now why don't we stop the clowning?" he said. "You boys know I'm all right. I know you're all right. We're all a little upset, but we're all big men. We can forgive and forget . . . and do business together."

Donald's narrow shoulders straightened unconsciously. Shake emitted a ponderous wheeze. "Now that's good sense," he declared. "Mighty good. Uh—what kind of business did you have in mind, Toddy?"

"Elaine was murdered for a watch. There was just one guy who knew I had it, the man that killed her. He's got rid of the watch by now. He'll also have an airtight alibi. So I'm stuck. All I can do is skip town . . ."

"This watch . . . did it belong to this guy in the first place?"

"No," Toddy lied. "It belonged to an old lady. I fast-talked her out of it. . . . God, Shake, I wish you and Donald could have seen the pile of stuff that woman had. Brooches, rings, necklaces. A good fourteen-fifteen grand worth or I don't know lead from platinum!"

"An' you just clipped her for the watch?"

"A *two-thousand-dollar* watch. I couldn't bite her any harder without raising a chatter. And, of course, I didn't dare go back for another try."

"Sure, uh-huh." Shake bobbed his jowls understandingly. "How come you hadn't turned the watch, Toddy?"

"Too hot. Milt wouldn't have touched it. I'd just about decided to take the stones out and cut it up for scrap, but I hadn't got around to it yet. I'd only had it three days."

"Mmm," said Shake. "Uh-hah!" he said briskly. "All right, Toddy, it's a deal. You just give us this old lady's address an' we'll see that you get your cut."

Toddy smiled at him.

"Now what's wrong with that?" Shake demanded. "We'll cut him in for a full half, won't we, Donald?"

"Well, it's been nice," said Toddy, rising. "I'll drop you a card from Mexico City."

"Now, wait a minute . . . !"

"I'll wait five minutes," said Toddy. "If I don't have two hundred bucks by that time, I'm on my way."

"Two *hundred!*"

"Two hundred—for almost a hundred times two hundred." Toddy's eyes flickered. "I won't say it'll be a cinch. She's about the crankiest, orneriest old bitch I ever tangled with. She lives all alone, see; doesn't have anyone she can pop off to. And she's got this game leg. I guess that makes her crankier than she would be ordinarily."

Shake licked his lips. "Game leg? An' she lives all alone?"

"Well," Toddy said conscientiously, "she *does* have three or four big Persian cats. I don't know whether they'd give you any trouble or not."

"I could handle 'em," said Donald grimly. "I could handle the dame. I ain't seen no dame or cats yet that I'm afraid of."

Toddy gave him an admiring look. Shake still hesitated. "How do I know you ain't lying to us?"

"Because you've got *brains*," said Toddy. "Elaine was murdered. Murders aren't done for peanuts. It all adds up. Donald sees it. You're as smart as Donald, aren't you?"

"Yeah, but—but—" The words Shake searched for would not come to him. "But two hundred!"

"Two hundred as of the present moment," said Toddy, glancing at his watch. "I just thought of another party I can go to who'll give me—"

"Two hundred!" Shake scrambled hastily from his chair. "It's a deal for two hundred!"

. . . Toddy sat in a quiet booth in the bar, sipping a Scotch and soda while he studied the classified ads in the evening paper. He was not content with what he had done. No revenge could be adequate for the brutal and hideous death Elaine had suffered. He had, however, done all he could. For the time being, at least, it would have to do.

He had felt for a long time that Shake and Donald

needed a lesson. Their threats tonight had done nothing to
ameliorate that impression. Now they would get that lesson, one they might not live to profit by, and Elaine's murderer, the chinless man—the "old lady" they expected to
rob—would get one. There'd be enough ruckus raised,
perhaps, to bring in the cops. It was too bad that Chinless
wouldn't know he'd been paid off, that Toddy had got
back at him. But nothing was ever perfect. He'd settled
two urgent accounts. He'd got a nice piece of scat money.
He'd done all that he could, and no man can do more.

He took out his billfold and, under cover of the newspaper, inventoried its contents. Three—three hundred and
twenty-seven dollars all together. Not very good. Not
when you had to buy some kind of car out of it; and he
would have to buy one. He had no way of knowing when
Elaine's body would be discovered. He did know that the
bus, plane and railway terminals would be watched as
soon as it was. They might be looking for him already. He
couldn't take any chances.

He slid out of the booth, sauntered past the bar stools
and out to the walk.

It was quite dark now, and the dark and the smog con-
densed the glare of neon signs to a blinding intensity. Still
he saw. He had to see and he did, although nothing in his
manner indicated the fact.

He strolled straight to the curb, his attention seemingly
fixed on the large wire trash basket which stood there. He
dropped the newspaper into it and stared absently at the
large black convertible. It was no more than ten feet away,
parked in the street with the motor idling. The back seat
was empty. The girl was at the wheel. The talking dog sat
hunkered at her side, his front paws on the door.

With an effort Toddy suppressed a shudder.

He saw now that he hadn't really taken a good look at

the dog that afternoon. The damned thing wasn't as big as he'd thought. It was bigger. And his imagination hadn't been playing tricks on him; it *did* talk.

The girl beckoned to Toddy. "Come," she called softly. The dog's jaws waggled. They yawned open. "C'm," he said. "C'm, c'm, c'm . . ."

Toddy looked over them and through them. He turned casually and stood staring into the bar. No way out there. The place had a kitchen, a busy one, and the rear exit lay beyond it. Up the street? Down? Pawnshops. A dime store. A butcher shop. All closed now.

He heard the softly spoken command in Spanish. He heard the scratch of the dog's claws as it leaped.

9

In one swift motion Toddy stooped, grabbed the base of the basket, and lofted it behind him. Either his luck or his aim was good. There was a surprised yelp, the rattling scrape of wire. But Toddy heard it from a distance. He rounded the corner and raced down the gloomy side street.

It was not good, this way, but no way was good. He was entering a semi-slum section, the area of flyblown beaneries, boarded-up buildings, flophouses and wine bars which lies adjacent to the Union Station. No cab would stop for him here.

So now he ran. Now for the first time he knew the real terror of running—to run without a goal, to be hunted by the upper world and his own; to run hopelessly, endlessly, because there was nothing to do but run.

Sweat was pouring from him by the time he reached the end of the street. And just as he reached its end he saw a huge black form, a shadow, whip around its head . . . The dog on his trail, behind him; the girl circling the block to head him off. That was the way it would be. He'd have to get in someplace fast. In and out. Throw them off. Keep running.

The dusty windows of a deserted pool hall stared back at him blankly. Next, a barber shop, also dark. Next, a burlesque house.

Across the grimy front, cardboard cutouts of bosomy women. Purple-eyed, pink-haired women in flesh tights and sagging net brassières. Sprawled beneath them and gazing lewdly upward, the cutout of a man—putty-nosed, baggy-trousered, derby-hatted. Names in red and white paint, Bingo Brannigan, Chiffon LaFleur, Fanchon Rose, Colette Casitas. And everywhere on streamers and one-sheets and cardboard easels, the legend: "Big Girl Show—DON'T DO IT SOME MORE."

"Yessir, the beeg show is just starting!" A cane rattled and drummed against the display. "Yessir," intoned the slope-chested skeleton in the linen jacket. "Step right in, sir."

He coughed as he took Toddy's ten-spot, but there was no surprise in it. He had always coughed; he could not be surprised. "Yessir"—he was repeating the instructions before Toddy had finished them—"Split with the cashier. Haven't seen you. Close the door."

"Exit?"

"Tough." The skeleton coughed. "Over the stage."

Toddy went in, anyway. It was too late to turn back. He moved past the half-curtains of the foyer and stood staring down the long steep aisle.

Not that he wanted one, but there didn't seem to be an empty seat in the joint. It was packed. Twin swaths of heads, terrazos of grays and blacks and bald-pinks stretched from the rear of the house to the orchestra pit. In the pit there was only a piano player, banging out his own version of the "Sugar Roll Blues." It must have been his own; no one else would have had it.

Toddy's nose crinkled at the stench, a compound of the aromas of puke, sweat, urine and a patented "perfume disinfectant." All the burly houses used that same disinfectant. It was the product of a "company" which, by an odd coincidence, also manufactured stink bombs. It was the only thing that would cover up the odor of a stink bomb.

He went slowly down the aisle, ears strained for sounds of the danger behind him, eyes fixed on the stage. Three chorus "girls" were on it—the show's entire line, apparently. They were stooped over, buttocks to the audience, wiggling and jerking in dreary rhythm to the jangling chords of the piano.

As Toddy advanced, the women straightened and moved off the stage, each giving her rear a final twitch as she disappeared into the wings. A man in baggy pants and a red undershirt came out. In his exaggerated anxiety to peer after the girls, he stumbled—he appeared to stumble. His derby flipped off, turned once in the air, then dropped neatly over his long putty nose.

Laughter swelled from the audience and there was a burst of hand clapping. The comic removed the derby and spat into it. He pulled the baggy pants away from his stomach and went through the motion of emptying the hat into them.

"Keep our city clean," he explained.

More laughter, clapping, stamping feet.

"Mi, mi, mi," chortled the comic, tapping his chest and coughing. "With your kind indulgence, I shall now sing that touching old love song, a heart-rending melody entitled (pause) 'If a Hen Lays a Cracked Egg Will the Chicken Be Nutty?'"

Laughter. A chord from the piano.

Toddy swung a foot to the pit rail and stepped across to the stage. The comic stared. He grasped Toddy's hand and wrung it warmly.

"Don't tell me, sir! Don't tell me. Mr. Addison Simms of Seattle, isn't it?"

No laughter. It was over their heads. Beneath the grease paint, the painted grin, the comic scowled. (*"What you pullin', you bastard?"*) "Why, Mr. Simms," he said aloud— simpering, twisting. "We can't do *that!* Not with all these people watching."

Howling laughter; this was right up the audience's alley. The scowl disappeared. The comedian released Toddy's hand and flung both arms around him. Head cuddled against Toddy's chest, he called coyly to the audience:

"Isn't he dar-ling?"

(*"How do I get out of here?"*)

"Don't you just lah-ve big men?"

(*"Dammit, let go!"*)

"You won't hurt me, will you, Mr. Simms?"

Above the whistling roar of the crowd, Toddy heard another sound. In the back of the house a brief flash of light marked the opening of the door. . . . A shouted, distant curse; the stifled scream of a woman. Toddy tried to jerk free and was held more tightly than ever.

"Kee-iss me, you brute! Take me in yo-ah ahms and—*oof!*"

Toddy gave him another one in the guts for luck, then a stiff-arm in the face. The comedian stumbled backwards. Stumbling, waving his arms, he skidded across the top of the piano and fell into the audience.

Over his shoulder, Toddy got a glimpse of people rising in their seats, milling into the aisle. He did not wait to see more. He darted into the wings, ducked a kick from a brawny man in an undershirt, and gave a blinding back-handed slap in return. A chorus girl tried to conk him with a wine bottle. He caught her upraised arm and whirled her around. He sent her sprawling into another girl—a big blonde with a pair of scissors. The third girl whizzed a jar of grease paint at him, then fled screaming onto the stage.

The exit was locked. He had to give it two spine-rattling kicks before the latch snapped. He stumbled out into the night, wedged a loaded trash barrel against the door—*that wouldn't hold long*—and ran on again.

He came out of the alley onto another side street. And

this was more hopeless than the first one. No lights shone. Several of the buildings were in the process of being razed. The others were boarded up.

He started down it at a trot, panting, nervous sweat pouring into his eyes. He ran wearily, and then his head turned in an unbelieving stare and he staggered into a doorway. There was a double swinging door with small glass ports on either side. Through the ports drifted a dim, almost indiscernible glow. He went in.

He was looking up a long dimly lit stairway, a very long stairway. What had once been the second floor was now boarded off. Except for the former second-floor landing, the stairs rose straight to the third floor.

Gratefully, he saw that the swinging doors were bracketed for a bar; not only that, but the bar was there, a stout piece of two-by-four, leaning against the wall. He picked it up and slid it into the brackets. He put a foot on the steps. The boards gave slightly under his tread, and somewhere in the dimness above him a bell tinkled.

He hesitated, then went on. A man was standing at the head of the stairs. He had a crew haircut and a mouthful of gum and a pair of pants that rose to his armpits. He also had a sawed-off baseball bat. He twiddled it at his side as he stared at Toddy with incurious eyes.

"Yeah, Mac?"

"Uh—I want to see Mable," said Toddy.

"Mable, huh? Sure, she's here. Agnes and Becky, too." The man chuckled. He waited, then jerked his head impatiently. "You can't jump 'em on the stairs, Mac. That's the only way they won't do it, but they won't do it that way."

Toddy ascended to the landing. He reached for his wallet, and the man moved his hand in a negative gesture. "Just pay the gal, Mac . . . Now, le's see . . ."

Doors, perhaps a dozen of them, extended the length of

the hallway. Doorways with half-doors—summer doors—attached to the outer casing. The man nodded, pointed to a patch of light.

"Ruthie's free. Go right on down, Mac."

He gave Toddy's elbow a cordial push; then his arm tightened on it in a viselike grip. "What the hell's that racket?"

"Racket?" said Toddy.

"You heard me. You bar that door down there?"

"Why the hell would I do that? . . . Wait a minute!" said Toddy. "I had to boot a wino out of the doorway to get in. He must have come back again."

The man cursed. "Them winos! And the goddam cops won't do a thing about them!" He headed down the stairs scowling, twirling the sawed-off bat. Toddy moved away from the stairwell.

There was no window at either end of the hall. There was nothing to indicate which of the rooms opened on the fire escape. There'd be one, surely, even in a whorehouse. But he'd have to hunt for it.

Come on, gizmo, he thought. *Be good to me.*

He rapped once, then entered the room the man had indicated. He hooked the summer door behind him. He grinned pleasantly as he closed and locked the other door.

"Hi, Ruthie," he said. "How've you been?"

"How you, honey?" She made a pretense of recognizing him. "Ain't seen you in a long time."

She might have been twenty-five or ten years older, depending on how long she'd been at it. Red-haired. Piled together pretty good. She wore sheer silk stockings, high-heeled black pumps and a black nylon brassière. That was all she wore.

She was sitting on the edge of the bed, shaving her calves.

"You mind waitin' a second honey? I kinda hate to stop an' start all over again."

"Let me help you," said Toddy promptly.

He took the razor from her hand and pushed her gently back on the bed. He said, "Sorry, kid," and snapped his free fist against the point of her chin.

Her eyes closed and her arms went limp. Her feet slipped from the mattress, and he caught and lowered them to the floor.

Stepping to the window, he ducked under the shade and looked out. Wrong room. The fire escape opened on the next one. He might—but, no, it was too far. He could barely see the damned thing. Trying to jump that far in the dark would be suicide.

Ducking back into the room, he stepped to the tall Japanese screen and moved it aside. There was a low door behind it, a door blocked by a small bureau. Toddy almost laughed aloud at the sight of it. A bureau joint, for God's sake! He'd thought that gimmick had gone out with "Dardanella." Probably it had, too. This one probably wasn't used any more . . . but it might still be working.

In this little frammis, one of the oldest, you were persuaded to leave your clothes on the bureau . . . You see, honey? No one can touch 'em. The door swings in this way, and the bureau's in front of it. You can see for yourself, honey . . .

Toddy pulled out the top drawer and laid it on the bed. Reaching into the opening, he found the doorknob. Would the dodge work from this side, that was the question. If it didn't—

The knob turned slowly. There was a quiet *click*. Then, a little above the level of the bureau, the mortised panels of the door parted and the upper half swung toward him.

The head of a brass bedstead blocked the doorway on the other side. The man in it stared stupidly through the rails at Toddy. He was a young man, but he had a thick platinum blond beard. Or so it seemed. Then, he raised his head, bewilderedly, and Toddy saw that the hair spread out on the pillow beneath him was a woman's.

"F-for gosh sake!" the man gasped indignantly. "What kind of a whorehouse is—"

Toddy's hand shot out. He caught the guy by the back of the head and jerked it between the bedrails.

The man grunted. The platinum hair stirred frantically on the pillow to an accompaniment of smothered groans. Toddy gave the bed a push. It slid forward a few inches, and he entered the room.

He stepped out the window, and stared down the fire escape. He took two steps, a third. The fourth was into space. Except for his grip on the handrail, he would have plunged into the alley.

He drew himself back, stood hugging the metal breathlessly. . . . Should have expected this, he thought. Building's probably been condemned for years. Now . . . He looked upward. No telling what was up there, but it was the only way to go.

All hell was breaking loose as he started up again. Doors were slamming, women screaming, men cursing. There was the thunder of overturning furniture—of heavy objects swung wickedly. And with it all, of course, the fearsome threatening snarl of the talking dog.

Suddenly, arms shot out of the window and clutched at Toddy's feet. He kicked blindly and heard a yell of pain. He raced up the remaining steps to the roof.

Stepping over the parapet, his hand dislodged a brick, and he flung it downward, heard it shatter on the steel landing. He pushed mightily with his foot, and a whole section of the wall went tumbling down. That, he thought, would give them something to think about.

Slowly, picking his way in the darkness, he started across the roof. There was no way out on either of the side streets he had been on. That meant he'd have to try for something on the parallel thoroughfare—up at this end, naturally, as far as he could get from the burly house.

He bumped painfully into a chimney, stumbled over an abandoned tar pot. He paused to flex his agonized toes and shake the sweat from his eyes. Unknotting his tie, he stuffed it into the pocket of his coat and swung the coat over his arm.

He was almost to the street now, and the majority of the buildings should be occupied. At any moment, he should be coming to a roof-trap or a skylight where—*Ooof!*

Glass shattered under his feet; there was a flash of light. He tried to throw himself backward and knew sickeningly that it was too late. He shot downward.

With a groaning wirish *whree* something caught his body in a sagging embrace. It hugged, then shoved him away. Upward. He landed on his side, unhurt but badly shaken. He opened his eyes cautiously.

He was lying on the floor beside a metal cot—a cot which, obviously, would never be slept in again. Down this side of the room and along the other were rows of other cots. At one end of the room, easily identifiable despite the half-partitions around them, were shower stalls and a line of toilets.

A flophouse, Toddy thought. Then he noticed the multitudinous chromos on the walls—GOD IS LOVE . . . JESUS SAVES . . . THE LORD IS MY SHEPHERD . . . and he amended the opinion. A mission flophouse. Heb. 13:8.

He got up and brushed the glass from his clothes. Picking up his coat, he crossed to the other side of the room and looked out a window. The stale air and the almost complete absence of light told him what he could not see. An air shaft. He'd have to go out through the door at the end of the room, and, if he knew his missions, there'd be plenty of people to pass.

Pondering drearily, desperately, a hope born of utter hopelessness entered and teased at his mind. Maybe Chinless *hadn't* got to Elaine. Maybe he didn't want to get Toddy. He might not have missed the watch. He might— uh—just want to talk to him.

Oh, hell. Why kid himself? Still, the idea wasn't completely crazy, was it? Elaine's murder had taken careful timing, a complete disregard for danger on the part of the murderer. Anyone as ruthless and resourceful as that would not waste time with dogs. Not if they wanted to bump you.

Chinless must have missed the watch. He'd missed it and he was holding off on killing him, Toddy, until he got it back. He—but wait a minute! If Chinless had got to Elaine, he already had the watch! Why else would he have killed—

"Is this right, brother?" said a severe voice. "Is this how we live in God's way?"

The man wore that look of puffed elation which seems to be the trademark of do-gooders, an expression born of a conscious constipation of goodness; of great deeds and wondrous wisdom held painfully in check; a resigned look, a martyred look, a determinedly sad look—a perpetual bitterness at the world's unawareness of their worth, at the fact that men born of clay take no joy in excrement, regardless of its purveyor. The man had a thick, sturdy body, a bull neck, a size six and five eighths head.

He gripped Toddy's arm and marched him swiftly

toward the door. "Don't do this again, brother," he warned.
"The physical man must be provided for, yes. We recognize the fact. But before that comes our duty to God."

Toddy made sounds of acquiescence. This guy obviously wasn't used to having his authority questioned.

They went down a short flight of stairs which opened
abruptly into a small sweat-and-urine-scented auditorium.
Tight rows of wooden camp chairs were packed with the
usual crowd of mission stiffs—birds who were too low,
lazy or incapacitated to get their grub and flop by other
means.

The man shoved Toddy into a chair in the front row,
gave him a menacing glare, and stepped to the rostrum.

"I apologize for this slight delay, brethren," he said,
with no trace of apology. "For your sakes, I hope there
will be no more. You are not entitled to the comfortable
beds and nourishing food which you find here. They are
gifts—something given you out of God's mercy and goodness. Remember that and conduct yourselves accordingly. . . . We will rise now and Praise Him from Whom
All Blessings Flow."

He nodded to the woman on the platform, and her
hands struck the keys of the upright piano. Everyone rose
and began to sing.

There was a comedian immediately behind Toddy. He
liked the melody to the hymn, apparently, but not the
lyrics; and he improvised his own. Instead of "Praise Him
from Whom All Blessings Flow," he sang something about
raisin skins and holy Joe.

The next song was "Onward, Christian Soldiers," which
the comedian turned into a panegyric on rocks and boul-
ders, the padding, in his opinion, of mission mattresses.

Toward the end of the hymn, the preacher cocked his

head to one side and sharply extended his hand. The pianist stopped playing; the bums lapsed into silence.

"Someone here—" he said, staring hard at Toddy, "someone thinks he is pretty funny. If he persists, if he commits any further disturbance, I am going to take stern measures with him. Let him be warned!"

Toddy stared intently at the song book. There was a heavy silence, and then another song was struck up— "Nearer My God to Thee."

The comedian behaved himself this time, but some guy in the back of the house was sure giving out with the corn. He was gargling the words; he seemed to be trying to sing and swallow hot mush at the same time.

The preacher looked at Toddy. He stood on tiptoe and stared out over the congregation. They went on singing fearfully, afraid to stop, and the corny guy seemed to edge closer.

Toddy stole a glance up from his book. The preacher's mouth had dropped open. He was no longer singing, but his hand continued to move through the air, unconsciously waving time to the hymn.

Then, at last, the owner of the preposterous voice came into Toddy's view. He sat down at his side, on the floor, and laid his great pear-shaped head against Toddy's hip. Having thus established proprietorship, he faced the rostrum, opened his great jaws to their widest, and "sang":

"Nrrahhhh me-odd t'eeeee . . ."

He was best on the high notes, and he knew it. He held them far beyond their nominal worth, disregarding the faltering guidance of the piano and the bums' fear-inspired determination to forge ahead with the song.

"Nrrahhh t'eee," he howled. "Neee-rroww t'EEEE . . ."

There was a crash as the preacher hurled his hymnal to

the floor. Purple with rage, he pointed a quivering finger at Toddy.

"Get that animal out of here! Get him out instantly!"

"He's not mine," said Toddy.

"Don't lie to me! You sneaked him in here tonight! That's why you were skulking upstairs! Of course he's yours! Anyone can see he's yours. Now get him OUT!"

Toddy gave up. He had to. The guy would be blowing the whistle on him in a minute.

He turned and started for the door. The dog hesitated, obviously torn between desire and training. Then, with a surly I-never-have-any-fun look, he followed.

Toddy paused on the sidewalk and put on his coat. The dog nudged him brusquely in the buttocks. He walked toward the curb, and the front door of the convertible swung open.

Toddy climbed in, heard the dog thump into the back seat, and leaned back wearily.

"What the hell's it all about?" he demanded. "What do you want with me?"

"You will know very soon," the girl said, and she would say no more than that.

10

Up until he met and married Elaine Ives, Toddy's world, despite its superficially complex appearance, was remarkably uncomplicated. Sound and practical motives guided every action; whims, if you were unfortunate to have them, were kept to yourself. Given a certain situation, you could safely depend upon certain actions and reactions. You might get killed for the change in your pocket. You would never get hurt, however, simply because someone felt like dishing it out.

Thus, on his wedding night, as he pushed himself up from the floor and slowly massaged his aching head, he couldn't accept the thing that had been done to him. He couldn't see it for what it was.

She'd been playing, putting on a show for him. Obviously, she'd just carried the act a little too far. She couldn't have meant what she'd said, what she'd done. She just couldn't have!

"Gosh, honey," he said, with a rueful smile. "Let's not play so rough, huh? Now what kind of whiskey would you like?"

"I'm sorry, T-Toddy. I—" She choked and tears filled her eyes.

"Forget it," he said. "You've just had a little more excitement than you can take. I should have seen it. I shouldn't have made you beg for a drink after all you've been through."

That was the way the incident ended. It was the way a dozen similar ones ended during the next few months. He gave in, and with each giving in her charm became thinner, the pretense of affection a leaner shadow. Why bother with charm, with pretending something she was incapable of feeling? It was easier and more to her taste simply to raise hell.

Still, Toddy couldn't understand; he refused to understand. She'd married him. Why had she done that unless she loved him? He wouldn't accept the contemptuous explanation she gave—that marriage, even to a chump like him, was better than working. She couldn't mean that. How could she when he'd done nothing to hurt her and was willing to do anything he could to help her? The fact that she'd make such a statement was proof that she was seriously ill. And so Toddy took her to a couple of psychiatrists.

The first had offices in his own building on Wilshire Boulevard, and he charged fifty dollars for a thirty-minute consultation. He allowed Toddy to spend one hundred and fifty with him before curtly advising him to spend no more.

"Your wife is not an alcoholic, Mr. Kent," he said. "In alcoholic circles she is what is known as, to speak plainly, a gutter drunk. A degenerate. She could stop drinking any time she chose to. She does not choose to. She is too selfish. In a way, you are fortunate; she might have had a penchant for murder. If she had, she would probably pursue it as relentlessly as this will to drink."

The opinion of the second psychiatrist coincided pretty largely with that of the first, but he was longer in arriving at it. He spent much more time talking to Toddy than to Elaine, usually detaining him for an hour or so after each consultation. Toddy didn't mind. The guy was obviously a square shooter and interesting to talk to.

"Toddy," he said quietly one afternoon, the last afternoon they talked together, "why do you stick with her, anyway? I've told you she's no good. I'm sure you must know it's the truth. Why continue a relationship that can only end in one way?"

"I don't know that she's no good," said Toddy. "I know that she needs help, that I'm the only person—"

"She doesn't need help. She's been helped too much. She got along most of her life without you, and she can get along very well without you for the rest of it. The Elaines of this world have a peculiar talent for survival."

"Put it this way, then," said Toddy. "I married her for better or for worse. I'm not going to pull out—and, no, I'm not going to let her—just because things don't break quite the way I think they should."

The psychiatrist nodded seriously. "Now we're getting somewhere," he said. "We're approaching your real reason, at last. Let's examine it and see how it stands up. Your parents were divorced and your mother remarried. From then on, until you ran away, you lived in hell. The experience gave you an undying hatred of divorce. You made up your mind that you'd never do what your parents had done. All right. I can understand that attitude. But,"—he pointed with his pipestem—"it's ridiculous to maintain it in this present case. You're married to a virtual maniac. You haven't any children. Now stop living with the past, and use that intelligence I know you have."

"I—" Toddy shook his head. "What did you mean, Doc, when you said the marriage, Elaine's and mine, could only end in one way?"

"I don't think I'll tell you. I think it would make a greater impression if you told yourself."

"How do I go about doing that?"

"Well, let's start back with the time you ran away from home. Your reason for leaving, as I remember, was that one of the barn rafters had broken and struck your stepfather. You were afraid you might be held responsible for the accident, so you ran away."

"Well?" said Toddy.

"It was an accident," said the psychiatrist, "and yet you had a package of sandwiches, a lunch, all prepared. You were able to get away just in time to catch the evening freight out of town. . . . That, Toddy, is just about the most opportune accident I ever heard of."

Toddy looked blank for a moment; then he grinned.

"And so on down the line," the psychiatrist sighed. "You're easy to get along with; you'll suffer a great deal before you act. If you'd been treated fairly by your stepfather or the county attorney or that gambling house proprietor in Reno or the detective in Fort Worth or . . . But that isn't important. It's not what I'm talking about."

"What are you talking about?"

"You must know, Toddy: the fact that you can't admit the things you've done, even to yourself. At heart you're what you'd call a Square John. You're peaceful. You don't ask much but to be left alone and leave others alone. That's your basic pattern—and life hasn't let you follow that pattern. You've been forced into one situation after another where your strong sense of justice has impelled you to acts which were hateful to you . . .

"Get away from Elaine, Toddy. Get away and stay away. Before you kill her."

11

The chinless man chuckled softly and massaged his hands. "I present my proposition a little too fast, eh? It was not what you expected. I must apologize, incidentally, for the manner in which you were induced to return here. It seemed necessary. It was important that I talk to you, and I felt you might not respond to a simple request to call . . ."

He waited, beaming, apparently for Toddy to make some polite disclaimer. Toddy didn't. For the moment, at least, he was incapable of saying or doing anything.

"As you can see," Chinless continued, "I mean you no harm. Quite the contrary, in fact. Despite the perhaps regrettable preliminaries of our meeting, I mean to benefit you—and, of course, to benefit myself. I would like to have you believe that, Mr. Kent; that I hold nothing but the friendliest feelings toward you."

He paused again, his beady black eyes fixed on Toddy's.

"Well . . ." said Toddy; and his head moved in a vague half-nod.

"Good!" said the man promptly. "Now we will go into the matter in detail, take up details in their proper order. First of all, my name is Alvarado; I am known by that name. You, of course, are Todd or Toddy Kent . . . also known as T. Jameson Kent, Toddmore Kent, Kent Todd and various other aliases. As you can see, I took the liberty of looking into your record after your visit here this afternoon. It interested me very much. It is largely why I have prevailed upon you to make this second visit."

"I—" Toddy swallowed. "I see."

"As you have probably observed," Alvarado went on, leaning forward earnestly, "extra-legal careers seldom attract the type of men which their successful pursuit demands. A willingness to flout often-foolish laws, yes—that characteristic is so common as to be unnoteworthy. But much more than that is required. Such men as yourself are indeed rare. I do not flatter you, Mr. Kent, when I say that some episodes in your past reflect positive genius."

Toddy nodded again, his tense nerves relaxing a little.

"You find the dog disturbing, Mr. Kent? You need not. He is a working dog—quite harmless, actually, unless ordered to be otherwise."

"I was just wondering," said Toddy, "how you found out so much about me so fast."

"Nothing could have been simpler. A description of you, and a generous retainer, naturally, to one of the better private detectives. A brief check at the city license bureau. Then a few cautious long-distance calls here and there . . . By the way, Mr. Kent"—Alvarado chuckled—"I should not show myself around Chicago, if I were you."

"I don't intend to," said Toddy. "Now, about this proposition of yours—you'd better not tell me about it. I don't think I can take it."

"But . . . I do not understand."

"The police are looking for me. Or they will be before long. My wife was murdered tonight—strangled in our room at the hotel."

"Murdered?" Alvarado frowned. "Strangled in your hotel room? What time was this, Mr. Kent?"

"Early this evening. Between six-thirty and seven, approximately." Toddy forced a smile. "To tell the truth, I thought you did it."

"I? Why did you think that?"

"Whoever killed her took the watch. Since it was your

watch and you were the only one who knew I had it, I naturally thought you'd done it."

Alvarado stared at him in dead silence, the frown on his fish-pale face deepening. Then, unaccountably, the beady eyes twinkled and he laughed with genuine amusement.

"The watch was taken, eh? That is very funny. Ha, ha. You are very amusing, Mr. Kent. Like me you have a sense of humor. I am glad to know it!"

"But—now, wait a minute!" Toddy protested. "I—"

"I understand. Ha, ha. I understand very well. Perhaps for the moment, however, we had better continue with our business."

"But you—"

"As I was about to explain," Alvarado said firmly, "my original motive in having you investigated was precautionary. I wished to discover whether you were of the type to take the watch—with all it would reveal to the knowing— to the police. Happily, I found you were not. You have every reason to avoid contact with the police. That is right, is it not?"

"Yes, but—" Toddy gave up. He couldn't see why Alvarado thought the murder so funny. But since he did, that was that. For the moment, he wasn't in a position to question the chinless man. Right now, he was on the receiving end of the questions.

"Yes," he said, "that's right. I can't go to the police."

"As I so ascertained," Alvarado nodded. "And having done so, I invited you here. For some time, Mr. Kent, a change in the personnel of this organization—of one of the personnel—has been strongly indicated. In fact, I have recommended such a change. But since no substitute for the incumbent was available, the recommendation did not carry much weight. In you, I think, I have found that long-needed replacement."

"You say you recommended the change?" Toddy asked.

"Yes. My superiors are not in this country, and it is necessary to consult them on such matters. Within reasonable bounds, however, they will act on my recommendations."

"I don't know," said Toddy, casually. "I can't see any big money in running gold across the border. Not for the individual runner."

"That was not what I had in mind."

"Well. You know I'm not a goldsmith."

"I know."

"I see," said Toddy. "Who's your present supplier?"

"Really, Mr. Kent." Alvarado laughed. "But I do not condemn your curiosity. It would be a splendid thing to know, would it not?"

"That's the spot you're planning for me?"

Alvarado shrugged. "For large rewards, Mr. Kent, one must expect to take certain chances. Your history indicates a willingness to do so."

"Up to a point," Toddy qualified. "There's one thing I don't understand. How can you get enough scrap gold to keep this racket running?"

"Another secret. You will understand when it is necessary for you to."

"I—" Toddy spread his hands helplessly. "I just don't see much point in discussing it, Mr. Alvarado. It sounds like a good proposition—one I'd jump at, ordinarily—but I can't take it now."

"No?"

"No! My wife was murdered tonight. I'm the logical suspect. I can't show myself anywhere. If I could, I'd be hunting down the murderer."

Alvarado started to smile again. "Ah, yes. Your wife . . . the watch. Perhaps you had better give me the watch now, Mr. Kent."

"Dammit!" Toddy snapped. "I just got through telling you that—"

"You want to keep it, of course," Alvarado nodded, understandingly. "You would be unintelligent if you did not try to. I do not blame you in the least, but it is impossible."

"But I haven't—"

"It is a sort of pattern, a template, you see. Without it, our work here would be seriously delayed. So,"— Alvarado's eyes glinted fire—"the watch, Mr. Kent."

Toddy got to his feet, carefully holding his arms out from his sides. The dog rose also, turning an inquiring eye toward the chinless man.

"Go ahead and search me," said Toddy hoarsely. "I can't give you something I haven't got."

"Since you are willing to be searched, you obviously do not have it with you. You will please tell me immediately where it is."

"I told you! I don't know—it was stolen!" He moved back a step as Alvarado rose. "Good God, do you think I'd make up a yarn like that? I thought you'd killed her. That's why I tried to get away from the girl. I—"

"What you thought, Mr. Kent, was that I was a fool. I am afraid you still think so. . . . Did you dispose of it to that loan shark you visited—that petty racketeer? Or to that watch shop where you sell your gold? Carefully, now! I can discover the truth of your answer quickly enough."

"I've told you the truth," said Toddy simply. "I can't tell you anything more."

Alvarado's hand dipped into the inside pocket of his coat and emerged with a snub-nosed automatic. He held it pointing squarely at Toddy's stomach.

"This is embarrassing," he sighed, "as well as vastly annoying. Before telling me that your wife had been murdered, you should have made sure that I could not prove the contrary."

"Prove?"

"Now you will accompany me to the hotel and extricate the watch from wherever you have hidden it."

"The hell I will!" Toddy shook his head.

"Really, Mr. Kent," Alvarado grimaced. "You must know you are being preposterous."

"I know I'm not going to walk into a roomful of cops," snapped Toddy. "Not if I had a dozen popguns like that pointing at me."

The talking dog whined softly and looked up at them, then padded away unnoticed in the tension of the moment. Ever so little, the chinless man's eyes wavered. He moved back a step or two until he was no longer standing on the rug. He stamped his foot on the floor.

A door opened and clicked shut. There was a gasp and then the girl swept into the room.

"Alvarado! You promised me that—"

"Silence!" The word cracked like a whip. "I have not broken that promise yet. I would much prefer not to. Tell me . . . Where did you pick up Mr. Kent's trail tonight?"

"Why, I—I—" The girl looked at Toddy. "Didn't he tell you?"

"Answer me! Quickly, truthfully, and in complete detail!"

"I picked him up—him and the other man I told you of—about three blocks from the hotel. They were going south on Spring Street. As I told you, I had to circle a number of blocks, driving up and down before—"

Alvarado's hand jerked sidewise. The gun barrel whipped across the girl's breasts and back again.

"You were listening at the door, eh? You would remove Mr. Kent from the difficult position in which his stupidity has placed him? I will give you one more chance. Why was it, when you were given Mr. Kent's address, you were forced to pick him up several blocks away?"

"Because . . . he got away from me."

"Yes?"

"I . . . it was as I told you. He was leaving the hotel when I first saw him; that was at about six o'clock. I followed him from there to the watch shop, then back again. In my haste to park, I passed through a red light. A police officer saw me. He insisted on giving me a lecture, then on trying to arrange a later meeting . . ."

A rosy flush spread under the cream-colored skin, and her eyes lowered for a moment. "I do not know exactly how long it was before I got away. Perhaps twenty minutes. Perhaps a total time of thirty minutes elapsed before I parked the car and got up to Mr. Kent's room . . ."

"Go on. You knocked on the door. You tried it and found it unlocked. See? I save you the repetition of tiresome details."

"I went in. Mr. Kent was not there . . ."

"But the room was in great disarray, eh? You were shocked by its condition."

The girl shook her head.

"No," she said dully. "There was no disarray. The room was in quite good order."

"Now wait a minute!" Toddy exclaimed. "I left that room just—"

"Quiet, Mr. Kent. You will have ample opportunity to talk in a moment. I shall even assist you." Alvarado grinned at him fiercely, then nodded to the girl. "You say the room was in reasonably good order, Dolores? Surely, you are overlooking one very important item. Only a few minutes before—or so he tells me—the body of Mr. Kent's wife was in that room. Brutally murdered. Strangled with

her own stockings. Killed and robbed of the watch which
Mr. Kent had hidden in a dresser drawer . . . You recollect
it now, eh? You remember this shocking sight now that I
have refreshed your memory? The body of Mr. Kent's wife
was in the room, yes? Answer me!"

Poised at the front door, the Doberman turned his great
head and stared at them thoughtfully. Then he bellied
down at the threshold, moved his muzzle back and forth
across the lintel. A quiet, waiting purr ebbed up from deep
in his throat.

"Well? We are waiting, Dolores."

The girl hesitated a moment longer, her lip caught between her small white teeth.

Then she looked up. She spoke staring straight into
Toddy's eyes.

"No," she said. "There was no body."

12

Airedale Aahrens (Need Bail?—Call Airedale) let the telephone jangle for a full minute while he lay cursing bitterly. Then he kicked back the bedcovers, snapped on the reading lamp, and literally hurled himself across the room.

"George!" he howled into the wall telephone. "How many times do I gotta tell you I . . . Oh," he said, after a minute. "Well, okay, George. Send him up."

Unlatching the door, he slid his feet into house slippers and shuffled out to the kitchenette. He poured himself a glass of milk from the refrigerator and carried it back into the other room.

The door opened, and City Councilman Julius Klobb came in.

"Look," he said. "This Elaine Ives—Kent. You've got to have her in court in the morning."

"I do, huh?" Airedale took a sip of milk. "Who says so?"

"Yes—you—do! And I say so. And you know why I say it."

"She'll have to do her time?"

"Naturally. Part of it, anyway; until the heat goes off."

"Heat," said Airedale, sourly. "Nine grand he takes off of me last year and still we got heat. Maybe I ought to fix through a beat cop. Or one of them guys that cleans out the washroom. Maybe they could earn their money."

Councilman Klobb spread his hands. "That's not being reasonable, Airedale," he said reproachfully. "The lid's been off now for well over eighteen months. Almost two years now without the slightest kind of rumble. I can't help it if we have an opposition party and they squeeze out from under once in a while. Frankly, I wouldn't have it any other way and I know you wouldn't. It's what makes America great—competition—unceasing struggle—"

Airedale groaned. "Unceasing horseshit. Put it away, will you? Save it for the Fourth of July."

"You'll have her there?"

"If it has to be her. We couldn't throw 'em another chump?"

"Of course not. Twenty-three arrests in a year and she's never laid out a day. She's the one they'll tie into. You know what'll happen when they do. Good God, man, do I have to draw you a picture?"

He didn't have to, of course. Airedale had known what to expect from the moment Elaine's name had been mentioned.

In many cities, bail is set to approximate the fine for a misdemeanor, and its forfeiture automatically closes the case. Usually, however, often in those places where the practice is most thoroughly entrenched, there are periods when it becomes inoperative. Bail then gives the law-breaker his freedom only until court is held. And if he fails to appear he is considered a fugitive.

This, as Airedale well knew, must not be allowed to happen in Elaine's case. Obviously, the political opposition intended to use her as a broom in a thoroughly unpleasant house-cleaning. This woman, they'd say—they'd shout—has forfeited almost two thousand dollars in bonds. Where is that money? What is there to show for it? What besides a parcel of land which has already been obligated for twenty times its appraised value?

Airedale shook his head ruefully. To stave off an investigation, Elaine would have to face court on charges which, under adverse circumstances, could total up to months in jail and/or several thousand dollars in fines. She'd be sore as hell—which didn't trouble Airedale in the least. Toddy would be sore—and that did trouble him. Toddy had laid his money on the line. Now he wouldn't get anything for it. Airedale would return the dough he had paid, of course, but that wouldn't help much. Once a rap was squared, it was supposed to stay squared.

"How about this?" he said. "Can't we get our paper back and put up the cash in its place?"

"Would I be here if we could?" Klobb demanded. "Can't you see they planned this so we wouldn't have time to squeeze out?"

Airedale nodded. For Elaine to face court was bad, but the alternative was indescribably worse: to face it himself.

"Okay. I don't like it, but okay. She'll be there."

"Good." Councilman Klobb stood up. "Better get her on the phone right now, hadn't you?"

"Get her on the phone," mocked Airedale. "Yessir, that's all I need to do; just tell her to go down and turn herself in."

"But . . ." Klobb frowned. "Oh, I see."

"Do you see that door?" said Airedale.

Klobb saw it. Rather hastily, he put it to use. Airedale began to dress.

Some fifteen minutes later he stepped out of a cab at Toddy's hotel and went inside. He was acquainted with the room clerk. He was acquainted with practically everyone in a certain stratum of the city's society. The clerk winked amiably, and extended a hand across the counter.

"How's it goin', boy? Who you looking for?"

"Might be you, you pretty thing," said Airedale. "But I'll settle for Toddy Kent."

"Kent? I'm not sure that he's regis—Oh," said the clerk,

glancing at the bill in his hand. "Yeah, we got him. Want me to give him a buzz?"

"Not now. Is his key in his box?"

"That don't mean nothing. People here carry their keys mostly. He should be in, though, him and the missus both. I ain't seen 'em go out."

Airedale deliberated. He had a deputy sheriff's commission but he was reluctant to use it. It was always much better, particularly when you were dealing with a friend, to have someone else do the strong-arm work.

"Where's old lardass, the demon house dick?"

"Up with some broad, probably. No, there he is,"—the clerk pointed—"in stuffing his gut."

Airedale glanced toward the coffee shop. "Okay, I'll drag him out. About three minutes after you see us catch the elevator, you ring hell out of Kent's phone."

Airedale got hold of Kennedy, the house detective, and together they went upstairs. They stopped at Toddy's door. Almost immediately the phone began to ring. It rang steadily for what must have been a full two minutes. There was no other sound, either then or after it had stopped.

Airedale raised his fist and pounded. He stood aside, and nodded to Kennedy. The house dick gripped the doorknob with one hand; with the other he poised a peculiarly notched key before the keyhole. He slowly turned the knob and pushed gently. He dropped the key back into his pocket, drew out a shot-weighted blackjack, and abruptly flung the door open.

"Okay," he growled, "come out of it!" Then, after a moment's wait, he went in and Airedale followed him.

They looked in the bathroom, the closet and under the bed. Panting from the unaccustomed activity and his recent meal, Kennedy dropped into a chair and fanned his face with his hat.

"Well," he said, "they ain't here."

"No kidding," said Airedale.

Airedale went to the window and looked out. He looked down at the once-white enameled sill—at the streaked outline of a heelprint.

Kennedy said, "She gave ol' Toddy a little more than he would take tonight. Boy, you could hear her yelling a block away!"

"Yeah?"

"I'm tellin' you, Airedale. It sounded like he was killin' her. If I'd had my way he'd of gone ahead and done it."

"So what did you do?"

"Gave him a ring. She'd already shut up by then, though, and there wasn't another peep after that."

Airedale stared in unwinking silence, and the house detective shifted uncomfortably. "Guess they must of gone out," he remarked, averting his eyes from the bondsman's liquid brown gaze. "Must of."

Absently scratching his nose, Airedale started for the window again, and his protruding elbow struck against the stack of the incinerator. He leaped back with a profane yell. Kennedy roared and pounded his knee.

"Oh, J-Jesus," he laughed. "You should of seen yourself, Airedale!"

"What the hell is this?" Airedale demanded. "A hotel or a crematory? What you got a goddam furnace goin' for in weather like this?"

Panting, shaking with laughter, the house detective explained the nature of the stack. Airedale made a closer examination of it. He kicked it. He removed a wisp of hair from the clamp. He measured the stack with his eye, and knew unwillingly that it was quite large enough . . . to hold a woman's body.

. . .

. . . Strolling back toward his hotel, he considered the smog through doggish eyes, reflecting, unsentimentally, that Elaine was doubtless part of it by now. That would be like her, to remain a nuisance even in death. Certainly it had been like her to get herself killed at such a completely inopportune time. When she failed to show in the morning, the cops would come after her. They'd do a little investigating, a little talking here and there, and the dragnet would go out for Toddy.

There was an all-night drugstore on the next corner. Airedale went in, entered a telephone booth and closed the door firmly behind him. He consulted a small black notebook and creased a number therein with his thumbnail. Fumbling for a coin, he checked over the contemplated project for possible pitfalls.

Fingerprints? No, they'd gotten her prints on her first arrest, and they hadn't bothered with them since. Pictures? No, they already had her mug, too, the newspapers and the police. And as long as she showed up in court—a woman of about the same age and size and coloring— Yeah, it could be done all right. Hundreds of women were in the Los Angeles courts every week. Elaine would draw the interest of papers and police only if she *didn't* show up.

Airedale dropped a slug into the coin box and dialed a number:

"Billie?"—he stared out through the door glass— "Airedale. How's it goin'? . . . Yeah? Well, it's slow all over, they tell me. . . . How'd you like a cinch for a while? . . . Oh, a buck—no, I'll make it a buck and a half. . . . Sure, don't you understand English? A hundred and a half a week. . . . Well, I'll have to talk it over with you personally. I don't like to kick it around on the phone . . . *Ex*penses? Sure, you get 'em, Billie girl. Board and room . . . absolutely free."

13

Toddy stared at the girl stonily. That reluctance of hers, the way she'd seemingly made Alvarado drag the story out of her, had been very well done. He'd almost believed for a moment that she was on his side. And now she'd lied. It *had* to be a lie. Either that or it was about time to wake up. It was time to give himself a pinch, put on his clothes, and go out for coffee.

With the body there in the room, the murder made sense. It put a frame on him like a Mack truck. Without the body, it was just plain damned screwy. It was nuts with a plus sign.

"Well, Mr. Kent?" Alvarado grinned satirically.

Toddy shook his head. "I've said all I've got to say."

"I see. Dolores, you will remain here. You, Mr. Kent, in front of me and through that door. I think you will be interested to see our basement."

"Wait!" The girl's voice was a sharp whisper. "Perrito, Alvarado! The dog!"

Alvarado looked. His gaze moved sufficiently from Toddy to take in the front door. He asked a soft question in Spanish.

¿Hombres, Perrito? ¿Sí, hombres?"

Eyes shining with excitement, the dog took a few prancing steps toward him. His jaws waggled with the effort to articulate.

"¡Bueno, perro!" said Alvarado. "Stand!"

The dog became a statue—a waist-high ebony menace pointed motionlessly toward the door. "The lights, Dolores . . ."

Alvarado moved behind Toddy, jabbed and held the gun against his back. The lights went off. Dead silence settled over the room.

It was like that for minutes. Absolute silence except for the restrained whisper of their breathing. Then, distantly, from outside and overhead, came a soft *ping*. That, the cutting of the telephone wire, ended the silence. Having removed their sole danger, or so they thought, the prowlers were actually noisy.

There was a scraping of feet against wood, a noisy thud. Footsteps clattered across the porch. A whining, scratching sound marked the slashing of the screen.

The door shivered. The knob turned, and out of the darkness came a profane expression of pleased surprise. Feet scuffled. The door clicked shut again.

The lights went on.

Shake and Donald stood side by side on the threshold. Their eyes blinked against the light. Then they ceased to blink, grew wider and wider in their greenish-white faces.

"J-j-j-jjjjj . . ." said Donald.

Shake's pudding head wobbled helplessly. Oscillating, he sagged back against the door.

Alvarado's icy voice snapped him ludicrously erect.

"Take three steps forward! Now lock your arms behind you! Dolores—" He jerked his head.

The girl went in back of the two men. She searched them with contemptuous efficiency. Donald, of course, was equipped with his long thin-handled knife. From Shake's hip pocket she withdrew a man's sock, weighted and knotted together at the top. She was about to toss it to the floor when Alvarado held out his hand.

"If you please . . . " He hefted the sock, grinning at the two thugs as he moved slightly away from Toddy. "The chicken claws, eh—the sock loaded with broken glass. To what do I owe this honor, gentlemen?"

"It—that don't really hurt mister," Shake blurted foolishly. "W-we wouldn't—"

"I am familiar with its possibilities. I wonder if you would still maintain it doesn't hurt if I should swing it vigorously against your crotch?"

Shake turned a shade greener.

Donald pointed an angrily indignant finger at Toddy. "He's the guy you ought to do it to, mister! He got us to come here!"

"Did he, indeed?"

"Just ast him if he didn't! Told us they was an old lady livin' here all by herself—an old crippled dame with a pile of jewelry!"

"That's just what he done, sir," Shake chorused righteously. "Got us to give him two hundred dollars for tippin' us off."

Alvarado glanced quizzically at Toddy. Toddy shrugged.

"I see. You,"—nodding at Donald—"is that what you were discussing with him earlier this evening?"

"It ain't *all* we was discussing." Donald eyed Toddy venomously. "What we was really discussing was murder. We—that's how we happened to make the deal with him. He killed his wife and he needed the money to blow town on."

"Oh, now," Alvarado laughed. "Murder his wife? I find that hard to believe. Doubtless he only told you that as a means of obtaining your money."

"I tell ya, he killed her! Anyways," Donald qualified reluctantly, "she got killed. She was layin' on the bed—right there in his hotel room!"

Alvarado made a sound of disbelief. "He invited you

up to pay your respects, I suppose? At what time was this?"

"Right around six-thirty. An', no, he didn't invite me up there! I sneaked up while he was out, see? I was gonna cut him up when he came back."

He babbled on eagerly, anxious to make the evidence against Toddy as damning as possible. Shake tried to interrupt him once; he seemed to sense that there was much more here than met the eye. A cold word from Alvarado, however, and Shake was reduced to flabby quaking silence.

Donald concluded the recital with a vicious leer at Toddy.

Slowly, the chinless man turned to the girl. "Well?"

"I told you what I saw. There is nothing more I can say."

"So," sighed Alvarado, "we are confronted with two contradictory truths. Apparently contradictory, I should say. I wonder . . . But we must not bother these gentlemen with out petty problems. They are obviously men of large affairs. We must speed them on their way—with, of course, some small memento of their visit."

He moved, smiling, toward the two. "You would like to leave it that way, gentlemen? After all, breaking and entering is a very serious crime."

They nodded vigorously.

Alvarado's smile vanished. "I will do you a favor. Turn around!"

"B-but—"

"I withdraw the favor!" He swung the sock—once, twice. He dropped it and grabbed the dog by the collar. "The blood scent arouses him, gentlemen. I advise you to run very fast."

They stared at him stupidly; dazed, not grasping his

meaning. The blows had reddened their faces. There was no other sign of their impact.

Then it came, the blood. It spurted out from ten thousand pinpoint fountains, formed into hideous red-threaded masks. The dog snarled and lunged.

"Quickly!" snapped Alvarado, and there was no doubting the urgency of his voice.

Shake and Donald came alive simultaneously. They hurled themselves at the door and wedged there. Clawing and cursing hysterically, they broke free. They stumbled and fell down the steps. The sound of their frantically pounding footsteps receded and vanished into the night.

Alvarado closed the door and stood with his back to it. He smiled at Toddy as he delivered a firmly admonitory kick in the dog's ribs.

"I seem to owe you an apology, Mr. Kent. I wonder if you will be generous enough to forgive and forget—if, in short, you are still of a mind to accept the offer I made you earlier."

Toddy's brow wrinkled. "Maybe. But what about my wife? Regardless of what's happened to the body, my wife's absence is going to be noticed. It's just a matter of time until the police will be looking for me. I can't show myself. I don't see how you can afford to be tied up with me."

"I am planning, Mr. Kent, to absolve you of the murder. Naturally, you would be of no use to me otherwise."

"You're *planning*?" Toddy said. "But how—why?"

"How I cannot yet tell you. As to the why, I have a double reason. Not only do I wish to have you associated with me, but I think it highly possible that the murderer may be my enemy as well as yours." Alvarado held up his hand. "Please! For the present, there is little more that I can tell you. And you have not accepted my offer . . . or have you?"

"All right." Toddy made up his mind. "It's my only chance. You've got yourself a boy."

"Good. Now, who knew that you had the watch?"

"You did."

"Of course. And Dolores. But who else? You told your wife about it, naturally?"

"No. Neither her nor anyone else."

"You are positive of that? Did you say anything to anyone which might, even by a remote chance, lead them to suspect that you had the watch?"

"No, I—" Toddy paused doubtfully.

"Did you or not? This is easily as important to you as it is to me, Mr. Kent."

"I talked to the man I sell gold to." Toddy gave him a brief summary of his conversation with Milt. "It couldn't have meant anything to him. Anyway, my wife was killed at just about the time I was talking to him."

"Then he is of no interest to us. It is as I thought. . . ."

"Yes."

Alvarado nodded absently. "Yes, it must be so. . . . But sit down, Mr. Kent. Would you like some coffee?—fine, so would I. Dolores!"

Toddy sat down and lighted a cigarette. Alvarado waited until the kitchen door had closed before he spoke.

"I will tell you something," he said quietly, "and please do not ask me to elaborate at this time. I place no great confidence in Dolores. Do not trust her too far."

"I don't trust anyone very far," said Toddy.

"Excellent. She is an attractive girl and not, I am afraid, above using her attractions. But, to get back to the matter at hand—when you discovered your wife dead and this man Donald fleeing down the fire escape, did you begin your pursuit of him immediately?"

"Of course."

"You made no search of the room?"

"I told—" Toddy interrupted himself with a startled curse. "Hell's bells! The guy could have been there for all I know!"

"Yes. He could still have been there when Dolores looked in. But do not blame yourself too much, Mr. Kent. You acted quite normally."

The kitchen door opened and Dolores came in with the coffee.

"None, thank you." Alvarado waved aside the cup the girl extended. "Pour Mr. Kent's, and then bring me my hat. After that, you may retire."

"I would prefer to remain up," Dolores said.

"It will be bad for your health to do so. Very bad. You will be amazed at the promptness with which the damage will manifest itself."

She gave him a sullen, baffled glare, but she turned and went out. Alvarado snapped his fingers at the dog.

"I will take Perrito with me, Mr. Kent. You will doubtless be able to rest better if you are alone."

Toddy said, "Thanks," and poured more coffee in his cup as man and dog left the house. Setting the enameled pot back on the serving table, he lighted another cigarette. He heard the car pull out of the driveway.

He took a sip of the coffee and let his eyes droop shut. Actually, he supposed there wasn't much use in thinking. He couldn't be guided by it except to a very limited degree. Until Elaine's murder was cleared up, it was strictly the chinless man's show.

Elaine. . . . He held the word in his mind, turned it over

and around; stubbornly, dully terrified, he refused to recognize the emotion which the name conjured. . . . *Hatred,
relief, now that she was dead?* Nonsense! He could have
got a divorce. He could have let her get one, as she'd wanted
to of late. He might feel that she was better off dead, but
that didn't mean—And wasn't he doing everything he
could to track down her murderer? Wasn't that proof
that—proof of how he really felt? He was doing everything he could to lay hands on the guy who killed her. That
was his only reason for stringing along with Alvarado. Of
course, the latter's offer was unusually attractive, the kind
of thing he'd been looking for. . . .

Only one setup could be prettier—to find out who the
present supplier was. He'd be loaded, stooped down with
dough he wasn't supposed to have.

"Mr. Kent!"

Dolores was kneeling beside him, the silken fullness of
her breast pressing against his arm. The blue V-necked
nightgown cast seductive shadows along the creamy planes
of her flesh.

"The coffee—you have been doped. You must leave
here at once!"

14

Toddy was a happy awakener; it was the one characteristic which had maddened Elaine more than any of his others. Shaking with a hangover, sick at her stomach, she would look at him in the morning and profanely demand what the hell there was to grin about.

So he looked at Dolores now, smiling not for her but himself. And then awareness came to him, and with it the chronic suspicion and hardness which life had engendered in him. But the smile still lingered, deceptively trusting and innocent.

"How's that?" he asked. "What do you mean, the coffee's doped?"

"You saw he did not drink of it? Now you must go!"

"Why?"

"You are in great danger. I cannot tell you more than that."

"Sure," said Toddy. "Sure, I'll go. Just as soon as you tell me how to dope black coffee. I've heard of almost everything, but I've never heard of that. There ought to be a fortune in it."

"B-but I—I—"

Her mouth closed helplessly over the words which had seemed so adequate a moment ago. He looked like a different man now. The mold remained the same but the contents had undergone a fearsomely rapid change. The soft crinkles of his smile had assumed the rigid hardness of ice.

"Well?"

"All right," she said, coloring. "I lied about the coffee. But—"

His hand closed suddenly over her arm. With a movement too swift to analyze, she was twirled up and around and smacked down upon his knees.

"You don't mind?" he said. "I like to look at people when I talk to them. Always look at people when you talk to them, and you won't have to wear false teeth."

"I—*let me*—!"

She tried to fling herself forward . . . and his right foot swung with casual expertness. She fell back into the hollow of his knees, her feet swept from under her. She balanced there foolishly, fury slowly surrendering to a growing fear.

"A little bony, aren't they?" he nodded. "You said I was in danger; I'm willing to be convinced. What danger?"

"It—the danger is not from Alvarado."

"Well, then?"

"That is all I will say."

"Oh, now," Toddy drawled, "we can't leave it there. We just can't do that. You haven't got a twin sister, have you?"

"A twin? I do not understand."

"Uh-huh. Some girl that looked just like you chased me all over hell tonight; hunted me down with a dog the size of a Shetland pony. I had my legs run off. I damned near got killed two or three times. And after the dog had caught me and herded me into her car, she brought me out here— the last place in the world I wanted to go. I tried to bribe her. I tried to argue with her. It was no soap right on down the line. And after all that, she turns pal on me. She's my bosom—no offense, honey—friend, I'm supposed to—"

"Please! If you'll give me a chance . . ."

"You've got it."

"I had to bring you here. I could not let you escape. Alvarado would have accepted no excuse."

"Why didn't you take it on the lam? Why don't you

now—if you really don't like the game? Alvarado's not in any position to make much trouble and neither are you. You'd be even-stephen."

He waited, eyebrows raised, watching the shivering rise and fall of her breast. There were tears in her eyes. She looked pathetically sweet and helpless and baffled, like a child who has had its hands slapped in the act of presenting a gift.

"I'm still here," he said harshly. "Let's have it."

"You!" she snapped, her eyes suddenly tearless, "you are so full of your own image that you can see nothing else! Are you blind? Have you forgotten that I tried to protect you tonight? I could have received much more than a blow. To make my story conform with yours, I—"

"Uh-huh. After it wouldn't do any good. After you'd already told him another one. . . . Did you ever get worked over by the cops, honey? It's pretty cute. You're in a soundproof room, see; you're buried where no one can get to you; you're not even booked, maybe. There's not a thing you can do but take it, the slaps, the hose, the kidney kicks; and you've had more than you can take hours ago. And then the door slams open and a nice fatherly guy comes in, and he gives these guys hell. They can't do that to you. He won't stand for it. He's going to get 'em all fired. Cute? Why, you'll fall on his neck—if you haven't been through the routine before."

"Oh," said Dolores, softly. "You think that—yes, you would have to think that. You could not be expected to think otherwise."

"Bingo, gin and blackjack," Toddy said. "Let's see if we can't agree on something else."

"I had better go. There is nothing I can say to you."

"How many times were you in my room tonight?"

"How—Why, once!"

"And the room was in order?"

"Yes! It was in order and I did not move the body—why in the world should I?—and you can believe that or disbelieve it and—*and I hate you!*"

"Sit still!" Toddy grabbed her arm and drew her back. "I haven't got much more to say but I want to be sure you hear it. My wife was a tramp. They don't come any lower. But I didn't want her dead, I particularly didn't want her dead that way. . . . No one deserves to die like that, alone, gagged, and strangled in a sleazy room in a third-class hotel. If I live long enough, I'll get my hands on the party that did it. When I do . . ."

"Surely, you cannot think that—"

"Think it?" Toddy shook his head. "I don't even think that you're trying to steer me away from my one chance to find the murderer. I don't even think that I might find myself in trouble if I picked you up on that steer—if I tried to leave. I don't think a thing. All I know is that hell's been popping ever since I came to this house this afternoon, and you've been right in the middle of the fireworks. I don't think a thing, but I don't *not* think anything either. That's the way it is, and as long as it is that way here's a tip for you. Don't toss that pretty little butt toward me again. If you do, I'll kick it for a field goal."

He put a period to the words with a knee jerk. It sent her stumbling to her feet, and she wobbled awkwardly for a moment, startled, furious, fighting to regain her balance.

"*You!*" she flung over her shoulder, and the door banged shut on the word.

She was none too soon . . . if it wasn't an act. For Alvarado had returned; a car was pulling into the driveway. Toddy wondered what line you took in a case like this.

If it was the chinless man's way of testing him, there was

only one thing to do. Tell him about it. It wouldn't hurt the girl; it would hurt him, Toddy, if he didn't.

If, on the other hand, she had given him a warning or a threat, the chinless man should still be told. He and Chinless were riding the same boat temporarily. What hurt one was very apt to hurt the other.

So he had every reason to speak of this, the girl's attempt to make him leave. But he couldn't quite make up his mind to do it. He still hadn't when, a moment later, Alvarado and the dog came in.

15

The dog came directly to Toddy and hunkered down in front of him. With the air of one nagged by a worrisome problem, he gazed studiously into Toddy's face.

"Nrrrah?" he said. "Nrrrah . . . t'ee?" Obviously the song both haunted and tantalized him. He could neither forget it nor recall the melody.

Toddy grinned despite, or, perhaps, because of his own serious situation. It was a relief to encounter something in this house so wholly undevious and understandable. He was humming the refrain of the hymn when a curt command from Alvarado interrupted.

Lugubriously, the dog moved away. Chinless dropped into a chair, rubbing his hands. He was feeling very pleased with himself, Chinless was. His shark's grin stretched from ear to ear.

"You have had some rest? Ah, yes, I can see you have. I see,"—he took an exaggerated sniff of the air—"that you have not been alone either. The girl lost no time in approaching you."

"Maybe." Toddy couldn't smell any perfume and he didn't think Alvarado could. It wouldn't mean anything, anyway, since she'd been in the room all evening. "Maybe," he said casually. "She could have been in while I was asleep."

Alvarado chuckled. "I understand. It has been years since such matters interested me, but I understand well. She is an attractive girl. You have lost your wife—"

"Just," said Toddy, "just a few hours ago."

"My apologies. My remarks were entirely out of order."

"All right," said Toddy.

"In rejoicing one is apt to become tactless, and I have reason to rejoice, Mr. Kent. We both do. The police may not be on your trail yet, but they soon will be. There is no question about it."

Toddy stared at him incredulously. "That's supposed to be good, is it?"

"Oh, very good. It—wait, please. I shall be glad to explain. I could not seriously doubt your story tonight; not after it had been confirmed by two men who obviously hated you. But my believing was not enough. My principles would demand more than that. So, I got more, much more than I expected."

He chuckled gleefully again, then hurried on at Toddy's frown. "I registered for a room at the hotel in the same wing yours is in. It was my intention to persuade the bellboy to let me look into yours—perhaps on the pretext that I smelled smoke coming from it. I had no way of knowing what I would find, if anything, but I felt certain that—"

"Get on with it," Toddy broke in impatiently. "You did get in. What did you find?"

"But I did *not* get in. Such was not necessary. The door was open and there were men inside. Detectives, beyond a doubt. I could only see one of them, and I could overhear only a snatch of their conversation. But that was sufficient. They were looking for your wife. Patently, they had been informed of her disappearance."

"But"—Toddy frowned—"that means the body *is* gone."

"Yes, it is very strange," murmured Alvarado, lowering one eyelid in a wink. "Very, very strange. Who would have a motive for removing the body? Not the murderer, certainly. To do so would conflict with his reason for committing the murder. So . . ."

"You're forgetting just one thing," said Toddy. "I didn't know the body was missing. I thought it was still there in my room."

"Did you, Mr. Kent?"

"Yes!" snapped Toddy, and then he shrugged and lowered his voice. "Let it ride. Let's have the rest of it."

"Good," Alvarado nodded sagely. "The point is a delicate one and there is really no point in discussing it. What matters is that your wife was killed—and I know the identity of her murderer. Please!" He held up his hand. "We can have no great amount of time to act. You had best let me explain in my own way.

"When I first missed the watch this afternoon, I notified our gold-supplier immediately. I did so reluctantly. As I have indicated, the man is no friend of mine. I detest him, in fact, and the feeling is reciprocated. Under the circumstances, however, I had no choice. He has many contacts in the gold trade; you might try to dispose of the watch. Such a potentially disastrous attempt had to be stopped at all costs."

"I don't see—"

"You will, Mr. Kent. Not only is this man my enemy, but he has long been anxious to withdraw from this organization. He will not say so, of course. He is afraid to. He knows that when we are willing to dispense with a man's services we also dispense with him—permanently. As long as our organization was functioning, and unless we chose otherwise, he would have to remain part of it.

"So this afternoon, today, he saw his opportunity. We presented it to him, you and I. By killing your wife, he would force you into summary action against me to establish your own innocence. Inevitably the facts of our organization would be brought to light. It would be impossible for us to operate, if ever, for a very long time. . . . That is why your wife was killed, Mr. Kent. So that this man might avenge himself upon me and free himself of an association which has become distasteful to him."

Toddy frowned dubiously. "I don't know," he said, slowly. "It seems to me like he had his own neck out pretty far."

"Not in his opinion. Like many persons who confess to cleverness, he is inclined to overlook the fact that others may be shrewd also. He felt certain, no doubt, that I would never see through his plan."

"Only you and they know who he is, is that right?"

"That is correct." Alvarado smiled sympathetically. "You have a right to know also, and you shall very shortly. I must lay the matter before my superiors and wait for their instructions, but that is a mere formality. The man will pay for his crime. There is not the slightest doubt about it."

"How?"

"Well"—the chinless man pursed his lips—"I imagine he will become conscience-stricken, Mr. Kent. Remorse will compel him to confess to the murder—in writing, of course—after which he will commit suicide."

He grinned mirthlessly. Toddy hesitated.

"I still don't see," he said. "I don't see why your people would go to such trouble to soak the guy. My wife meant nothing to them. He tried to get you, but you were trying to get him, too. He's never said he wanted to pull out of the racket, and—"

"I will tell you why," Alvarado interrupted. "Our work is sponsored by my government. It is a poor government, financially speaking, and an unpopular one; a ragged pariah among the commonwealth of nations. It must have gold to survive. It can get gold in this way. Lately, there have been indications that it might be able to secure loans from this country. There is much sentiment against them here, but there is some cause for hope. Can you imagine what would become of that hope if I, an agent of this already unpopular power, was charged with murder? With specifically the murder of a woman and an American citizen?"

"Yes," Toddy nodded, "I can."

"You Americans are a peculiar people, Mr. Kent. You are undisturbed by what amounts to mass murder, but let one of you be killed—a woman, in particular—and your entire nation is one voice demanding vengeance. . . . That is why this man will be severely and promptly punished. For actually jeopardizing the security of my government for his own purposes."

"Can you prove that he did?"

"I shall be able to. Within the next twenty-four hours, I hope. And please do not ask me how; I cannot tell you. In the meantime . . ."

"I'd better hide out?"

"Yes. It may not be necessary, but we can take no chances. We do not know what the police have been told. It is dangerously futile to guess. Tijuana will be safe. I have contacts there."

With a muttered word of apology, Alvarado took a bus timetable from his pocket and held it up to his eyes. He studied it, squinting, for a moment, then fitted a pair of steel-rimmed spectacles to his nose and peered at it again. Abruptly he thrust it toward Toddy.

"Will you examine this abominable thing? The fine print—even with glasses I cannot read it."

Toddy repressed a smile; the print wasn't particularly fine. "Sure," he said. "What are we looking for?"

"I thought it would be best to depart from one of the suburban stations. If you will select one, I will drive you there. I would take you all the way to Mexico, but to do so, I am afraid, might endanger both of us."

Toddy's finger traced down the columns of print, and paused. "How about Long Beach?"

"That should do, I think. When does the next south-bound bus leave from there?"

"Two o'clock." Toddy glanced at his wristwatch. "About an hour from now."

"Then we had better be going. On the way I will tell you what you must do when you reach Tijuana." Alvarado rose and reached for his hat. "You have money, I believe. Good! . . . Come, Perrito."

16

Bathed, shaved and wearing the freshly pressed clothes and the new shirt the bellboy had brought up, Toddy sat on the bed of his San Diego hotel room and poured out the last of his breakfast pot of coffee.

The bus had arrived at six o'clock. It was now almost eight. Except for Elaine's death and his own precarious position, he would have felt pretty good. He actually felt pretty good despite those things. He had a sensation of being at peace with himself, of being able to relax after a lifetime of tension. He was not tired—he felt invigorated, in fact—yet there was a strong desire to sit here and rest. Just rest and nothing else.

And he knew that the quicker he got out of this town, the better off he'd be.

San Diego's unique semi-tropical climate was not the only thing it was noted for. Nor its great aircraft plants, nor Navy and Marines bases. Among the denizens of the world to which Toddy belonged, it was also known as a swell place to steer clear of. Its vagrancy laws were the harshest in the country. To be "without visible means of support"—a surprisingly elastic category in the hands of local cops and judges—was a major crime. In the same month here a vagrant—an unemployed wanderer—and a woman who had murdered her illegitimate baby were given identical prison sentences.

Despite the earliness of the hour, a crowd of holidayers was already waiting for the bus to the Mexican border. Toddy hesitated, thought for a moment of making the seventeen-mile trip in a cab. There'd been nothing about Elaine's death in the morning papers; apparently, there was no alarm out for him. Still—he took his place in the waiting line—he couldn't be sure. It was best to stick with a crowd.

He stood up throughout the thirty-minute ride to the border. The bus unloaded, there, on the American side, and he made himself one with the mass which crowded through the customs station.

He had no trouble in crossing the international boundary. The busy United States guard barely glanced at him as he asked his nationality and birthplace. The Mexican customs officers did not bother to do even that much. They simply stood aside as he and the others filed past.

Toddy climbed into a Mexican taxicab, jolted over a long narrow bridge, and, a minute or two later, stepped out on Tijuana's main thoroughfare. He strolled leisurely down it, a wide dirty street bordered by one- and two-story buildings which were tenanted mainly by bars, restaurants and curio shops.

It was a bullfight day, and the town was unusually crowded. Americans jammed the narrow sidewalks and swarmed in and out of the business establishments. Most signs were in English.

Toddy walked to the end of the street, to the turn which leads off to the oceanside resort of Rosarita. Then he crossed to the other side and walked slowly back. Near the center of town, he turned off onto a side street and strolled along for a few doors. He passed a curio shop, lingeringly, then paused and went back.

He entered.

The shop was stocked to the point of overflowing. Racks of beadwork, leather goods and trinkets jammed the aisles. It was almost impossible to squeeze past them.

Once past, it would be impossible to be seen from the street.

A fat Mexican woman was seated on a campstool just inside the door. She beamed at Toddy.

"Yess, please? Nice wallet? Nice bo'l of perfume for lady?"

"What have you got in the way of gold jewelry?" Toddy asked. "Something good and heavy?"

"*¡Nada!* Such things you could not take across the border, so we do not sell. How 'bout nice belt? Nice silver ring?"

"Oh, I guess not," said Toddy. "Not interested in anything but gold. Real gold."

"You look around," the woman beamed, placing her campstool in front of the door. "I get nice breath of air. You may find something more nice than gold."

Toddy nodded indifferently, and squeezed his way back through the racks. A few feet, and the display suddenly ended; and a Mexican man sat on a stool against the wall, reading a copy of *La Prensa*.

He wore an open-neck sports shirt, sharply creased tan trousers and very pointed, very shiny black shoes. He was no more than five feet tall when he stood up, smiling, ducking his glossy black head in greeting.

"Mr. Kent, please? Very happy to meet you!"

He opened a door, waved Toddy ahead of him, and closed and locked it again. A courteous hand on Toddy's elbow, he guided him down a short areaway and into a small smelly room.

There was an oilstove cluttered with pots and pans, a paint-peeled lopsided icebox, a rumpled gray-looking bed. Toddy sat down at an oilcloth-covered table, smeared and specked with the remains of past repasts. His nostrils twitched automatically.

"The ventilation is bad, eh?" The Mexican showed gleaming white teeth. "But how would you? The windows must be sealed. The disorder is essential. Think of the comment if one in this country should live in comfort and decency!"

"Yeah," said Toddy uncomfortably. "I see what you mean."

The Mexican moved back toward the icebox. "It is nice to meet one so understanding," he murmured. "You will have bo'l of beer, yess? Nice cold bo'l of beer?"

Toddy shook his head; he hoped he wouldn't have to be holed up long in this joint. "I guess not. A little early in the day for—"

"No," said the Mexican. "You will have no beer."

There was not the slightest change in his humbly ironic voice. There was no warning sound or shadow. But in that last split second when escape was too late, Toddy knew what was coming. He could feel the gizmo's swift change from gold to brass.

The blow lifted him from his chair. He collapsed on the table, and the table collapsed under him. There was a muted crash as they struck the floor.

But he did not hear it.

17

Tubby little Milt Vonderheim was not Dutch but German. His right name was Max Von Der Veer. He was an illegal resident of the United States.

The only son of a good but impoverished Hessian family, he had been expelled from school for theft. Another theft landed him in prison for a year and caused his father to disown him. Milt learned the watchmaking trade in prison. He was by no means interested in it, but useful work of some kind was mandatory and it appeared the easiest of the jobs available. He was not sufficiently skilled at the time of his release to follow the trade.

He was not particularly skilled at anything, for that matter. And, after an unsuccessful attempt at burglary, which almost resulted in his rearrest, he became a waiter in a beerhall. He fitted in well there. He was lazy and clumsy, but this very clumsiness, coupled with what seemed to be a beaming, unquenchable good humor, made him an attraction. . . . That waiter, Max, *ach!* Snarling his fingers in the stein handles, stumbling over the feet he is too fat to see. A clown, *ja!* You should hear him when he tries to sing!

Since he could do nothing else, Milt put up with the gibing and jokes. He beamed and exaggerated his clumsiness, and made a fool of himself generally. Inwardly, however, he seethed. He had never been good-natured; he was sensitive about his appearance. He could have toasted every one of the beerhall customers over a slow fire and enjoyed doing it.

Then, one day, the leader of a troupe of vaudevillians

112

noticed Milt, and was impressed by what he saw. This awkward youngster could be valuable; he was a natural for low-comedy situations. He didn't have to pretend (or so the leader thought). He was a born stooge and butt.

Milt joined the troupe. Eventually, early in 1913, he came to America with it.

That was the end of the good-natured business. That was the end of being the clumsy and lovable little brother of his fellow vaudevillians. Cold-eyed and unsmiling, Milt let it be known that he despised and hated them all. One more innocent joke, one more pat on his ridiculously potted belly—and there would be trouble. The funny business was strictly for the stage from now on.

Milt got away with it for four months, during which he extorted three raises in pay. By the time he deliberately forced his dismissal, he had acquired a sizable sum of money and no small knowledge of the country, its language and customs.

He got himself fired in San Francisco. Five days and five hundred dollars later, he had a new name and a number of sworn documents proving his American citizenship. His parents, these documents revealed, had been the proprietors of a San Francisco restaurant. He had been privately tutored by a Dutch schoolmaster. Parents, restaurant, schoolmaster—and the original records of his birth—had been destroyed in the great fire and earthquake. Milt's English was not good—but what of that? Many legal residents of the country talked a poorer brand. For that matter, many legal residents of the country had no legal way of proving their right to be here except by the very method Milt used.

Americans, it seemed, were not as exacting as Germans, and Milt easily found employment as a watchmaker. He pursued it just long enough to discover that his employer's streak of larceny, while latent, was virtually as broad as his own. At Milt's suggestion—for which he took half the profits—the store owner filed hundreds of suits against merchant seamen for articles allegedly bought from him. Since the defendants had shipped out and were unaware of the notices of suit brought in obscure legal papers, judgment was automatic.

Later he opened his own small side-street watch-repair shop. Until a certain day in 1942, he thought he was doomed to remain there, barely making a living, a foolishly cheerful-looking fat man who could not acquire the wherewithal and was rapidly losing the nerve for the gigantic swindles he dreamed of.

One of these last was inspired by his own history. Perhaps there were many persons who had entered and remained in the United States under the same circumstances as his. If one had the means to ferret them out—! Ironically, he was pondering this very scheme on that day in 1942 when, looking up from his workbench, he discovered that others had thought of it also. Thought of it and acted upon it.

Being Milt, he was not, naturally, at all discomfited by the discovery. His words and his expression were actually contemptuous.

"Do not tell me, please!" He narrowed his eyes in mock thoughtfulness. "Ah, yes, I remember now. Madrid, 1911, was it not? Alvarado and his Animales. There was considerable debate, I remember, as to which was which."

"And, you, I recall you well, also," said the chinless man. "A human swine—there would have been a novelty! Unfortunately, my *pobres perros* rebelled at the thought. But—enough! Listen to me carefully, Herr Von Der Veer, and do not interrupt!"

He spoke rapidly for ten minutes, ending with a sharp-soft "Well?" that was a statement rather than a question. Milt took a drink from a brandy bottle before replying.

"Let me see if I understand," he said. "You have aligned your cause, unofficially, with that of the Reich where my father is now resident. And unless I accommodate you in this matter, certain unpleasant things will happen to him. He might possibly find himself in prison, that is right?"

"Regrettably, yes."

"Fine," said Milt. "Beat him well while he is there. Starve him also, if you can. He has such a great fat stomach I doubt that it is possible."

Milt smiled pleasantly. The chinless man blanched. "Monster!" he stammered, then recovered himself. "But there is something else, Herr Max. You are in this country illegally. A word to—"

"Any number of people," said Milt, truthfully, "will swear that I was born here. But why do we dispute, Señor Alvarado? That so-foolish man who leads your equally preposterous government—"

"Silence!"

"—may be moved by motives of idealism. You may be also. I am not so stupid. I want money. If you want this thing done, you will pay for it. It is as simple as that, and no simpler."

Thus, Milt, who like everyone else in the jewelry trade had begun dabbling in gold when the price went to thirty-five dollars an ounce—thus, funny-looking little Milt became a large-scale buyer for the Nazi government.

His first move was to build up a group of house-to-house buyers who worked out of his shop. Their purchases, less perhaps an undetectable third, went directly and regularly to the mint, where he built up and still had a reputation as a man above suspicion. His next move was to rent numerous post-office boxes under different names;

small boxes, such as individuals rent. Under those names, he inserted small newspaper ads in as many different sections of the country.

There are thousands of such advertisers; little men, often with little knowledge of a highly exacting business. Because they are little, they feel obliged to place money ahead of good will. They grade and weigh "close"—the doubts which always arise are decided in their own favor. Because they lack the necessary training and wit—and despite their petty and pitiful efforts to do the opposite—they make disastrous buys. It is then obligatory, or so they feel, to be still "sharper" to make up for their losses.

The end result of all this is that the little men acquire a bad or at best "uneven" reputation. They buy less and less gold. Usually, in a few months or a few years, they are out of business.

It would be a physical impossibility to check on all these small mail buyers, and the federal authorities see no need to do so. Before gold can be diverted into the black market, it must first be acquired. And the little men just don't buy it, not a fraction of the quantity needed to pay them for the risk. . . . That is, of course, none of them bought it but Milt's little men. Gold poured in on the little men. They bought pounds of it every day.

Milt had expected to get out of the gold traffic when the Nazis had become unable to buy. But the chinless man gave no sign of ceasing operations, and Milt was far too wise to express a desire to quit. Angrily he realized that, in effect, he was jeopardizing his liberty and perhaps his life for nothing. He could never spend his wealth in the United States. He would never be allowed to leave the United States to spend it. He was getting old. Unless he withdrew from the ring soon, it would be too late. The things money bought would have become meaningless.

Mixed with his anger was a kind of apathy, a dread dead feeling that whatever he did mattered little. Even if he could get away . . . well, what then? How would a man of his age occupy himself in a strange new country? Alone, completely alone, with no one to care whether he lived or died.

He had been unable to deposit his money in a bank and afraid to place it in a safe deposit box; such might attract attention, and what if he should have to leave town in a hurry? So, unobtrusively, he had had a small but excellent safe sunk into the floor beneath his workbench. It could be cracked, of course, as the best of safes can be. But what knob-knocker or juice worker or torch artist would suspect that Milt had anything worth getting?

None did. The idea was laughable. Milt used to laugh, smile a little sadly to himself, as late at night sometimes he examined the stacks upon stacks of large-denomination bills. So much money . . . for what?

So he had gone on, reasonlessly, because there was nothing else to do, and fate in time had brought Toddy and Elaine Kent to him. *Elaine!* There was someone like himself, a woman who thought as he did. With someone like her, with her and the money, life would at last be what it should. And why not have her? It was only a question of ridding her of her fool husband, and if she kept on drinking, making trouble—and if that was not enough, if Toddy would not leave her or permit her to leave . . .

Night after night Milt had brooded over the matter; cursing, thinking in circles, guzzling quart after quart of beer. And, finally, Toddy had stumbled upon the house of the talking dog; and from then on thinking almost ceased to be necessary. Every piece of the puzzle had fallen into place at the touch of Milt's stubby fingers.

True, there had been one slight hitch, a hair-raising moment when all seemed lost. But that was past, now. Nothing remained but the pay-off. There was no longer danger—or very little. Things had not worked out quite as he had planned, but still they had worked out.

The phone rang. Milt answered it, casually, then grinned with malicious pleasure:

"Yes, I did that, *Señor.* Something you should have done yourself. . . . Why? Because he was dangerous, a menace to us. At least that was my honest opinion. I have not acted out of venom—as our superiors will most certainly feel that you have. . . . Eh? Oh, you are mistaken, *mein Herr.* You have but to consult your morning paper—*The News.* The others did not see fit to carry the item. And if that is not enough for you . . .

"If you demand stronger proof"—Milt's voice dropped to a wicked caress—"pay me a visit."

18

A chilling, icy, weight enveloped Toddy's head. He tried to move away from it, but couldn't. It kept moving with him. From far away, in a dim fog-muted world, came the sound of voices. . . . A man and a woman, talking, or a woman and two men. . . . The voices came closer, some of them, then lapsed into silence. Something squeezed his left wrist, released it, and regrasped his right arm. The arm moved upward, and a probe dug painfully at the flesh. Then, fire flooded his veins and his heart gave a great bound, and Toddy bounded with it.

Eyes closed, he bounded, staggered, to his feet, and the icy weight clattered from his head. Then he was pressed back, prone, on the bed; and he opened his eyes.

A dark, neatly dressed man was staring down at him thoughtfully, slapping a hypodermic needle against the palm of his hand. Also gazing down at him, her dark eyes anxious, was the girl Dolores.

"It's all right, Toddy." She gave him a tremulous smile.

Toddy stared at her, unwinking, remembrance returning; then, swung his eyes toward the man with the needle.

"You a doctor?"

"Yes, *Señor.*"

"What's going on here? What happened?"

"I have given you an injection of nicotinic acid. To strengthen the heart. Lie still for another half hour, and keep in place the ice pack. You will be all right."

"I asked you what happened?"

The doctor smiled faintly, shrugged, and spoke rapidly

in Spanish to Dolores. Toddy's eyes drooped shut for a moment, and when he reopened them he was alone with Dolores.

"Well?" he said. "Well . . . ?"

"You should not talk, Toddy." She sat down on a chair at the bedside, and laid a hand on his forehead. "There is little I can explain, and—"

Toddy rolled his head from beneath her hand. "That guy tried to kill me?"

"To knock you unconscious. You were to be disposed of later . . . at night."

"Why?"

"I cannot tell you. There is much I do not understand."

"You know, all right. Why did Alvarado want me killed?"

"Alvarado did not want you killed."

"No? Then why—"

"If he had," said the girl, "you would be dead."

Toddy frowned, then grunted as a stab of pain shot through his head. "Yeah," he said. "But—"

"Try not to think for a few minutes. Rest, and I will make you some coffee, and then, if you feel able, we can leave."

"Leave?"

"Rest," said Dolores firmly.

Toddy rested, more willingly than he pretended to. It was almost reluctantly that, some fifteen or twenty minutes later, he sat up to accept the coffee Dolores prepared. She gave him a lighted cigarette, and he puffed and drank alternately. His head still throbbed with pain, but he felt alert again.

"So," he said, setting down the cup, "Alvarado doesn't want me dead?"

"Obviously not."

"He knew this was going to happen?"

"I think—I think he must have."

"What did he stand to gain by it?"

"I cannot say. I mean, I don't know."

"No?"

"No!" snapped the girl; but her voice immediately became soft again. "Believe me, Toddy, I don't know. But you will soon find out. Alvarado himself will tell you."

"Alvarado will!" Toddy started. "What do you mean?"

"That is why I am here, to take you to him. He is in San Diego."

Toddy fumbled for and found his cigarettes. He lighted one, staring at Dolores over the flame of the match. He didn't know whether to laugh or bop her. How stupid, he wondered, did they think he was?

"What's Alvarado doing in San Diego?"

"Again, I do not know."

"But after this pasting I got, I'm still supposed to see him?"

"So I told you."

"What if I refuse to go with you? What happens, then?"

"What happens?" The girl shrugged, tiredly. "Nothing happens. You are free to go your own way. You may leave here now, if you feel able."

Toddy shook his head, incredulously. "You say that like you mean it."

"I do. You will not be harmed. . . . Of course," she added, "your situation will not be exactly pleasant. You have little money. You are a fugitive. You are in a foreign country. . . ."

"But I'm alive."

"There is no use," said Dolores, "in arguing. I was not ordered to persuade you, only to ask you."

She stood up, walked to the battered dresser, and picked

up a flowered scarf. Draping it over her black hair, she knotted it under her chin and took a step toward the areaway.

"Good-bye, Toddy Kent."

"Now, wait a minute. . . ."

"Yes?"

"I didn't say I wouldn't go," said Toddy. "I just—Oh, hell!" He wobbled a little as he lurched to his feet, and she moved swiftly to him. He caught her by the shoulders, his hands sinking into the soft flesh with unconscious firmness.

"Look—" He hesitated. "Give me the lowdown. What had I better do?"

"I am here to take you to Alvarado."

"But should I—?"

"Suppose I said no; that you should remain in Mexico."

"Are you telling me that?"

"Suppose I did so advise you," Dolores continued, looking at him steadily, "and you decided to do the opposite— and repeated my advice to Alvarado?"

"Why would I do that?"

"You have no reason to trust me. In fact, you have made it very plain that you do not trust me. Why shouldn't you tell Alvarado? Particularly, if it appeared that by doing so you would help yourself?"

Toddy reddened uncomfortably and released his grip. The girl stepped away from him.

"I guess," he said, "I can't blame you for thinking that."

"No."

"But you're wrong. If I'd wanted to get you in trouble, I could have told Alvarado about—well—"

"—my warning to you last night? Perhaps you did, after you left the house."

Toddy gave up. She was dead right about one thing. He

didn't trust her, even though something had impelled him to for a minute. Perhaps she didn't know what Alvarado wanted. Or perhaps she did. He'd never take her word for it, regardless of the situation. Whatever she advised him to do, he'd be inclined to do the opposite.

"Where's my coat?" he said shortly. "Let's get out of here."

"You are going with me?"

"I don't know. Maybe a drink will help me to make up my mind."

. . . They went out the same way Toddy had come in, squeezing past the crowded racks of trinkets and curios. The little man who had slugged Toddy was nowhere in view. The fat woman was still seated near the doorway on her campstool.

"Nice bo'l of perfume for lady?" she beamed. "Nice wallet for gen'leman?"

Toddy started to scowl, but something about her expression of bland good-natured innocence made his lips tug upward. He gave her a cynical wink, and followed Dolores out the door.

It seemed like days had passed since he had arrived in Tijuana that morning, but the clock in the bar indicated the hour as five minutes of two. Seated in a rear booth, Toddy drank a double tequila sunrise and ordered another. He took a sip of it and looked across the table at the girl.

"Well," he said. "I've made up my mind."

"I see."

"I'm not going with you. I'll lay low here for a few days. Then I'll beat it back across the border and—" Toddy broke off abruptly, and again raised his glass. Over its rim, he saw the faint gleam of amusement in Dolores' eyes.

"On second thought," she said, "you will head south into Mexico. That is right?"

"Maybe," said Toddy. "Maybe not."

"I understand. It is best to keep your plans to yourself. Now, I must be going."

She slid toward the edge of the booth, hesitated as though on the point of saying something, then stood up. Toddy got up awkwardly, also. On an impulse, as her lips framed a mechanical good-bye, he held out his hand.

"I'm sorry about last night," he said. "I don't know where you fit into this deal, but I think you're playing it as square as you can."

"Thank you." She did not touch his hand. "And I think you also are as—as square—as you can be. Now I would like to tell you something. Something for your own good."

"I'm waiting."

"Wash your face. It is dirty."

She was gone, then, her body very erect, her high heels clicking uncompromisingly across the wooden floor. Toddy stared after her until he saw the bartender watching him. Then he shook his head vaguely, ran a hand over his jaw, and headed for the men's restroom.

It was at the rear end of the room, a partitioned-off enclosure inadequately ventilated by a small high window opening on the alley; a typical Tijuana bar "gents' room." There was a long yellowish urinal, and two cabinet toilets, flushed by old-fashioned water chambers placed near the ceiling. Adjacent to the two chipped-enamel sinks was a wooden table, supporting a sparse assortment of toilet articles and an elaborate display of pornographic booklets, postal cards, prophylactics and "rubber goods."

"Yessir, mister"—the young Mexican attendant came briskly to attention—"you in right place, mister. We got just what you—"

"What I want," said Toddy, "is some soap." And he helped himself from the table.

He turned on both water taps, scrubbed his hands, then lathered them again and scoured vigorously at his face. He rinsed off the soap and doused his head. Eyes squinted, he turned away from the sink and accepted the towel that was thrust into his hands.

"Thanks, pal." He dried his face and opened his eyes. "Don't mention it," burbled Shake.

"And keep your hands out o' your pockets," gritted Donald.

19

Toddy did not need the last bit of advice. One swift glance at the hideously scratched mugs of the pair told him they would kill him on the slightest pretext. Kill him and worry about the outcome later. Fury had made them brave.

Shake was holding a blackjack—upswung, ready to strike. Donald had the Mexican attendant backed against the wall, the point of his knife pressing against his throat. The door of the restroom was barred.

"Just don't try nothin'," murmured Shake. "Jus' don't try nothin' at all. You get past us, which you ain't goin' to do, I got two of my *pachucos* outside."

"Someone'll be coming back here." Toddy's voice sounded strange in his ears. "You can't keep that door barred."

"I c'n keep it barred long enough. Turn around."

"You tailed me down here?"

"What does it look like? Turn around!"

The blackjack came down sickeningly on Toddy's shoulder. He turned.

Shake slapped his pockets expertly, located his wallet, and extricated it with a satisfied grunt. There was a moment's silence, another grunt, and another command to "Turn around."

Toddy turned.

"What you doin' here?" Shake demanded. "What's the deal?"

"Deal?"

Donald ripped out a curse. "Let him have it, Shake. We can't wait here all day."

"No one's tryin' to bust in," Shake pointed out, his eyes fixed on Toddy. "I asked you what the deal was?"

Toddy licked his lips, wordlessly. Helplessly. The blackjack began to descend.

"*Wait!*" It was the Mexican attendant. "I will tell you, *Señores!*" His teeth gleamed at Toddy in a warm, placating smile, a grin of apology. "I am sorry, *Señor,* but it is best to tell them. These gentlemen mean business."

Donald nodded venomously. "You ain't just woofin', *hombre.* Spill it!"

"But you must know, gentlemen. What else would it be but—but—"

"But what?"

"White stuff," said Toddy, taking the Mexican off the limb. "As my friend says, what else could it be?"

Donald sneered. Shake gave Toddy a look of mock sanctimoniousness. "I might of knowed it," he said. "A man that'll murder his own sweet little wife an' play mean tricks on people that trust him won't stop at nothin'. Dope, tsk, tsk. You smugglin' it across the border?"

"Not at all," said Toddy. "I use it to powder my nose."

He fell back from the blow of the blackjack, and Shake advanced on him. "Okay," he wheezed. "Be smart. Be good an' smart. It's gonna cost you enough. Where you got the stuff hid?"

"I"—Toddy's eyes flicked around the room, settled momentarily on one of the elevated water chambers, and moved back to Shake—"I've got it cached out in the country a few miles."

"The hell you have—" Donald began. But Shake interrupted him.

"You give yourself away, Toddy. You're losin' your grip. Get up there an' get it."

"Up where?"

"You better move!"

"Okay," sighed Toddy. "You win."

With Shake at his heels, he stepped into the first of the toilet enclosures and gripped the top of its two partitions. He gave a jump, swung himself upward, and got a knee over one of the partitions. Grasping the pipe which ran from the flush chamber to the toilet, he pulled himself up until he stood straddling the enclosure.

Donald issued a curt command, and the Mexican hastened to lie down in the adjacent booth. Then the little shiv artist crowded in next to Shake, holding his knife by the blade.

"Don't try nothing'," he warned. "I can't reach you but the knife can."

"Yeah," said Toddy. "I know."

He gripped the ends of the heavy porcelain lid of the water chamber. Grunting, he moved it free and edged backward.

"Have to help me with this," he panted. "It's—"

"Now, wait a—" wheezed Shake. And Donald's knife flashed with the swift action of his hand. But he was too late. They couldn't stop what Toddy had started. They couldn't get out of the way.

"—heavy!" said Toddy. And he hurled the heavy lid downward with all his might.

It caught Shake full in his fat upturned face, one end swinging sickeningly against the bridge of Donald's nose. They sprawled backwards out of the enclosure, and Toddy scrambled down hastily from his perch.

He need not have hurried. The Mexican attendant, apparently, had exactly anticipated his actions. Now he was on his feet, administering one of the most thorough, expert yet dispassionate kickings that Toddy had ever seen. It was a demonstration that would have been envied even by Shake's *pachucos*.

Not a kick was wasted. Each of the two men received two kicks in the guts, by way of obtaining temporary silence. Each received a kick in the temple, by way of making the silence more or less permanent. Each received three kicks in the face as a lasting memento of the kicking.

"*¡Bien!*" said the Mexican, smiling pleasantly at Toddy. "I think that is enough, eh?" Then he bent over the motionless thugs, stuffed their wallets and Toddy's inside his shirt, and picked up the knife and blackjack.

"I have been put to much trouble," he beamed. "You do not mind the small present?"

"That money," said Toddy, "is all I have."

"So? You want it very much, *Señor?*"

"I guess not," said Toddy. "Not that much. . . . How do I get out of here?"

"The table, *Señor*. Drag it over to the window. . . . You will excuse me if I do not help? It is an easy drop to the alley."

Toddy nodded, dragged the table to the window, and stepped up on it—deliberately destroying as much of the display as he could.

"It is all right, *Señor,*" the Mexican laughed softly. "Everything is paid for."

"Yeah." Toddy grinned unwillingly. "What happens to these characters? And their *pachucos?*"

"People come back here," the Mexican explained, "but no one go out. So, soon, very soon, my father will be alarmed."

"Your father?"

"The bartender, *Señor*. He will summon my brother, the

waiter, who will call my two cousins, officers of the police. . . ."

"Never mind." Toddy hoisted himself into the window. "I know the rest. Your uncle, the judge, will give them ninety days in jail. Right?"

"But no, *Señor*"—the Mexican's voice trailed after Toddy as he dropped into the alley—"he will give them at least six months."

Toddy plodded down the alley to the street, lighted the last of his cigarettes, and threw the package away. He thrust a hand into his pocket, drew it out with his sole remaining funds. Sixteen cents. Three nickels and a penny. Not enough to—

A hand closed gently but firmly over his elbow. A blue-uniformed cop looked down at the coins, and up into his face.

"You are broke, *Señor?* A vagrant?"

"Certainly not." Toddy made his voice icy. "I'm a San Diego businessman. Just down here for a little holiday."

"I think not, *Señor.* Businessmen do not take leak in alley."

"But I didn't—" Toddy caught himself.

"For vagrancy *or* leak," said the cop, "the fine is ten dollars. You may pay me."

"I—just give me your name and address," said Toddy. "I'll have to send it to you."

"Let's go," said the cop brusquely, in the manner of cops the world over.

Toddy started to protest. The officer immediately released his grip, unholstered a six-shooter, and leveled it at Toddy's stomach.

"We do not like vagrants here, *Señor,* even as you do not like them in your country. A ver' long time ago I visit your country. I am a wetback, yes, but no one care. The lettuce must be harvest' and I work very cheap. Then I complain I do not get my wages an' I am sick from the food—*cagada,* dung—and everyone care ver' much. I am illegal immigrant. I am vagrant. I go to jail for long time. . . . It is good word, vagrant. I learn it in your country. Now move. *¡Anda!*"

The gun pointing at his back, Toddy preceded the cop down the side street, across the main thoroughfare, and so on down another side street. Tourists and sightseers stared after him—curiously, haughtily, grinning. Mexican shopkeepers gazed languidly from their doorways, the dark eyes venomous or amused at the plight of the *gringo.*

Toddy walked on and on, his jaw set, his eyes fixed on the walk immediately in front of him. He knew something of Mexican jails by reliable hearsay. When you got in down here, brother, you were in. The length of sentence didn't mean a thing. They took weeks and months, sometimes a year, to get around to sentencing you. They just locked you up and left you. And—*and Shake and Donald!* . . . Toddy's step faltered and the cop's gun prodded him. . . . There wasn't a chance that he could persuade the two thugs to play quiet. They'd squeal their heads off about Elaine's death and the supposed dope racket, and—

Somewhere a horn was honking insistently. Then a car door slammed, and Dolores called, *"¡Un momento!"*

The cop grunted a command to halt, and swept off his cap. *"¿Sí, Señorita?"* he said. *"A servicio de—"*

He didn't get a chance to finish the sentence, or any of the several others he started. After three minutes of Dolores' rapid Spanish, he was reduced to complete silence, answering her torrent of reprimand only with feeble shrugs and apologetic gestures.

At last she snapped open her purse and uttered a contemptuous *"¿Cuánto?—how much?"* The cop hesitated, then drew himself erect. *"Por nada,"* he said, and walked swiftly away.

Toddy said, "Whew!" and, then, "Thanks."

The girl nodded indifferently. "I must go now. You are going with me?"

Toddy said he was. "Shake and his boys were trailing me. I—"

"I know; I saw them enter the bar. That is why I waited."

"It didn't occur to you," said Toddy, "to do anything besides wait?"

"To call the police, for example? Or to intervene personally?"

"You're right," said Toddy. "Let's go."

As they neared the international border, Dolores took a pair of sunglasses and a checkered motoring cap from the glove compartment and handed them to him. Toddy put them on, glanced swiftly at himself in the rear-view mirror. The disguise was a good one for a quick change. Even if his mug was out on a pickup circular, he should be able to get past the border guards.

He did get past them, after a harrowing five minutes in which the car was given a perfunctory but thorough examination. He had to get out and unlock the trunk compartment. On the spur of the moment—since he had neglected to do so sooner—he had to invent a spurious name, birthplace and occupation.

He was sweating when the car swung out of the inspection station and onto the road to San Diego. As they sped past San Ysidro, he removed the cap and glasses, mopped at his face and forehead.

"I am sorry," said Dolores, so softly that he almost failed to hear her. She was looking straight ahead, her eyes intent on the road.

"Sorry?" said Toddy vaguely.

"You are right to be angry with me, to be suspicious. What else could you be? Except for me you would not have been involved in this affair."

Well, Toddy thought, she'd called the turn there. But what he said, mildly, was, "Forget it. I was asking for it. A guy like me wouldn't feel right if he wasn't in trouble."

"Wouldn't he?"

Toddy looked at her, looked quickly away again. She couldn't mean what she seemed to, not with Elaine murdered and himself the principal suspect. That, and everything else that was hanging over him. Of course, she wouldn't be any angel herself but . . . But he couldn't think the thing through. It was a hell of a poor time to try to.

"I don't know," he said shortly. "Probably not."

"I see." Her voice was flat.

"I"—Toddy hesitated—"maybe. It would depend on a lot of things."

20

The house was in the Mission Hills section of San Diego, located on a pie-shaped wedge of land overlooking the bay. On one side a street dropped down to Old Town. On the other side another road wound downward toward Pacific Highway. In the front, a multiple intersection separated the house from its nearest neighbor by a block. There were no houses in the rear, of course; only a steep bluff.

Toddy sat in the front room—a room as sparsely furnished as the one in Chinless' Los Angeles dwelling. He had been sitting there alone for some fifteen minutes. As soon as he and the girl had arrived, Alvarado had spoken rapidly to her in Spanish—too rapidly for Toddy's casual understanding of the language—and she had gone down the hallway toward the rear of the house. Alvarado had followed her, after politely excusing himself, and closed the door; and dimly, a moment later, Toddy had heard another door close. Since then there had been silence—almost.

It seemed to Toddy, once, that he heard a faint outcry. A moment later he had thought he heard the dog bark. *Thought.* He wasn't sure. He strained his ears, held his breath, listening, but the sounds were not repeated.

Toddy waited with increasing uneasiness. In the far corner of the room was a desk littered with papers. When he and Dolores had arrived, Alvarado had been working there, and something about the sight had given Toddy an inexplicable feeling of danger. He wanted to get a better look at those papers. He wondered whether he dared risk the few steps across the room and a quick glance or two.

He decided to try it.

Rising cautiously, an eye on the hall door, he tiptoed across the floor and looked swiftly down at the desk. The papers were covered with rows of neatly written figures, interspersed occasionally with what appeared to be abbreviations of certain words. They were meaningless.

"Meaningless, Mr. Kent," said Alvarado, "unless you have the code book."

He came in smiling, closing the door behind him, and crossed to the desk. He picked up a small black book that had been lying face down and riffled its pages of fine, closely printed type.

"This is it. Regrettably, it is much too complex to explain in the brief time we have."

"Better skip it, then," said Toddy, matching the other's irony. And as he resumed his seat on the other side of the room, Alvarado chuckled amiably.

"A man after my own heart," he declared, sitting back down at the desk. "I cannot tell you how disappointed I am that we shall not work together. . . . For the time being, at least."

"No?" Toddy crossed his legs. The air was heavy with perfume. Alvarado apparently had doused himself with it.

"No. Unfortunately. But we will come to that in a moment. I have had you visit me so that I might explain—explain everything that may be explained. You are entitled to know; and, as I say, I hope we may work together eventually. I did not wish you to be left with an unfavorable opinion of me."

"Go on," said Toddy.

"After I dispatched you to Tijuana, I communicated the fact to our supplier of gold . . . the man I suspected of killing your wife. He, reacting as I believed he would, ordered you murdered. To be slugged and disposed of permanently as soon as it was expedient. As soon as the first half of the order was carried out, I intervened. I had the proof I wanted."

"Proof?" Toddy frowned. "I don't get it."

"But it is so simple! He killed your wife—I was certain—merely as a means of disposing of you. He hoped to involve you, and through you me, in a crime which would break up our syndicate and release him from duties which have long been onerous to him. Now you understand?"

"No," said Toddy. "I don't."

"But it is—"

"Huh-uh." Toddy shook his head. "Up to a point, I'll buy it. He killed Elaine. I thought you'd done it. If I played the cards he gave me, I'd have either gone after you myself or hollered to the cops. . . . But I didn't do that. You and I squared our beef. He didn't have a thing to gain by getting rid of me in Tijuana."

"Hmmm." Alvarado drummed absently on the desk. "I see your point. It was stupid of me not to think of it. . . . Of course," he added, smoothly, "I was not completely sure of this man's motive. There was a strong possibility that he might have been motivated by revenge."

"Remember me?" said Toddy. "I'm supposed to be the bright boy. So stop kidding me. . . . This guy tried to get me killed; I'll go along with that. And when he did he proved that he'd killed my wife. Why? I'll tell you. Because he was sure that, given a little time, I'd be able to dope out who he was. You were sure I would, too, and, until you got your orders from abroad, you had to protect his identity. You had to pin the rap on him good before I did too much thinking."

"Really, Mr. Kent . . ."

"That's the way it was. That's the way it has to be. Now why beat around the bush about it?"

Alvarado stared at him thoughtfully, a quizzical frown

on his pale shark's face. Then, gradually, the frown disappeared and he nodded.

"Very well, Mr. Kent. I suppose there really is no longer need for secrecy. The man you mention has served us well . . . in the opinion of my superiors. He is now closing out his affairs and will soon be out of this country. Possibly—probably—we will find use for him elsewhere. But that is no concern of yours. Long before you can discover his identity and confirm it, he will be beyond your reach."

Amazement choked Toddy for a moment. He could hardly credit himself with hearing the words that Alvarado had spoken. Before he could find his voice, the chinless man was speaking again.

"I can well understand your confusion, Mr. Kent. I share it. But there is nothing I can do about it. Our entire hypothesis was wrong. This man we suspected did not kill your wife."

"You're lying!" Toddy snapped. "Murder or no murder, this guy is valuable to your bosses. They're going to protect him at all costs. That's the whole story, isn't it?"

"It is not. My bosses, as you call them, do not act so whimsically. The man was able to prove, irrefutably, that he did not kill your wife. As an unfortunate result, our superiors retain their original high regard for him while I— for the moment, at least—have been made to appear a clumsy and vindictive fool."

"You're forgetting your lines," Toddy said grimly. "A minute ago you were saying that—"

"I was speaking in theoretical terms. Like you, I was speeding down a trail of theory and I am at a loss when the trail disappears."

"My getting slugged wasn't any theory!"

"Be grateful you were not killed, and dwell no more on the matter. Nothing good will come of it."

Hands shaking, Toddy lighted a cigarette. After an angry puff or two he ground it out beneath his foot. Alvarado nodded sympathetically.

"You are annoyed. I am withholding information which you feel is vital to you. Does it occur to you that I might easily be annoyed with you for much the same reason?"

"I'm not holding back anything."

"Knowingly, no. And I am not doing so willingly."

"I don't," said Toddy, "get you."

"You yourself had the best opportunity to kill your wife. You had ample motive, also. You are not the type to kill with premeditation, but I can readily imagine your doing so in a moment of temporary insanity. And since such a crime is inconsistent with your nature, your conscious mind would refuse to admit it. . . . All this is conjecture, of course. I know nothing. I want to know nothing."

Toddy laughed shortly. "Tell me why I was slugged. Maybe I'll sign a confession, then."

"You invite the obvious retort, Mr. Kent. Tell me how you disposed of your wife's body and I will tell you why you were slugged."

Toddy stared at him helplessly. "You don't believe that," he said. "You know I didn't kill her. Maybe this guy, the supplier, didn't do it either, but—"

"He didn't."

"Then, what's it all about? What are you trying to steer me away from?"

Alvarado shook his head. Turning back to his desk, he opened the code book. "So that is the way it is," he murmured. "You will excuse me if I work while we talk."

Toddy started to speak; his hand started to knife out in a gesture of angry exasperation. The gesture was unfinished. He remained silent—staring, trying not to stare.

That code book was in unusually fine print. And yet

Chinless was studying it without difficulty and without his glasses. He couldn't be—shouldn't be—but he was. What the hell could it mean? Why had he claimed that his eyes were bad right from the moment of their first meeting? Why had he pretended that he couldn't read Milt's card? What reason was there—

"Now," said Alvarado, "let us leave theory to the theorists and take up practical matters. As I indicated, we are ceasing activities in this country indefinitely; but we hope to resume them. When that time comes we can find a profitable place for you. . . ."

"Suppose I don't want it?"

"That is up to you. We have no fear of your talking."

"All right," said Toddy, "I'm listening."

"There is a Pullman train leaving here tonight; what you call a through train. I have reserved you a stateroom. It will not be necessary for you to leave that stateroom until you arrive in New York. You will be given a thousand dollars in addition to your passage. That should maintain you in some degree of comfort until I get in touch with you."

"How will you do that?"

"A detail. We will work it out before you leave. Does the idea, generally, please you?"

"It doesn't look like I have much choice," said Toddy. "I want to know why you're jumping the country, though. I'm hot enough without getting any hotter."

"You will not be. I, at this point, am the sole recipient of the heat. The informer in our midst has chosen to make no mention of you to the authorities."

"Informer? Who is he?"

"That need not concern you." Alvarado turned a page of the code book and ran a pencil down the column of symbols. "This informer is one of our unwilling operatives. We were able to obtain his"—Alvarado slurred the pronoun—"cooperation through a brother, a political prisoner in one of my country's excellent labor camps. It was necessary for the brother to die. Our confederate discovered the fact through a relative. He made the very serious mistake of confronting me and charging bad faith."

Toddy nodded, absently. He was staring at the code book, at Alvarado. Something warned him to look away, but he couldn't. "I see," he said. "You knew he'd turn stool pigeon."

"He already had," grimaced Alvarado, "though I was unaware of it until yesterday. I had assumed that his tirade against me was immediately subsequent to the news of his brother's death. Then, through a slip of the tongue, he revealed that he had known of it for a month. He had known of it but said nothing, continued the regular course of his affairs, until his sense of outrage overcame his discretion. Obviously, he had done so for only one reason. . . . You followed me, Mr. Kent?"

Toddy didn't speak. Alvarado looked up from the desk.

"I am boring you, perhaps?"

"What?" Toddy started. The answer had come to him at last, at the very moment of Alvarado's question. A beautifully simple yet almost incredible answer. "I don't quite get it," he said, with forced casualness. "This guy has squealed. Why haven't the Feds moved in on you?"

"Because they hope to trap the man who supplies our gold. He is to meet me here—or so I advised our informer—tomorrow night. The efficient T-men will not come near the place, nor do anything else to arouse my suspicions, until then."

Toddy nodded absently, his mind still working on the riddle of Alvarado's "bad eyesight." . . . Let's see, he thought. Let's take it from the beginning. I gave him that frammis about a friend sending me to him, and then I gave him the card. He let me into the house. Then . . . well, I didn't have much to say for a minute or two, and he began to freeze up a little. Asked me my business. Said he couldn't read the card. He must have, but—

Toddy started slightly. *Why, of course! Chinless had thought he'd been sent there to the house. When he discovered the truth, that their meeting was sheer accident, he had pretended that . . .*

The chinless man looked down at the code book. He looked up quickly, and his gaze met and held Toddy's. A frown of regret spread over his dead white face.

"Well?" said Toddy.

"It is not well," said Alvarado, and his hand dipped into his pocket and came out with the automatic. "You have an expressive face. Like our informer, Dolores, it tells too much."

21

Toddy forced an irritated laugh. "What the hell's the matter with you anyway? What have I done now?"

"It is not so much what you have done. It is what you surely would do . . . now that you know. I am sorry. I, personally, am sorry you cannot do it. But I have my orders. The man must be protected."

"I still don't know—"

"Please!" Alvarado gestured fretfully. "You know and I know you know. In a little while, a few weeks, it would not have mattered. The man would have vanished. You, I believe, would have grown more philosophical about the matter. Now—"

"About murder?" Toddy dropped his mask of bewilderment. "Why would I stand still for a murder that this guy committed?"

"He did not commit one. At least, he did not kill your wife."

"But—All right," said Toddy. "He didn't. I did. Is that good enough?"

"Not nearly, Mr. Kent. You are certain that he did kill her. You would act accordingly. There would be much talk—many secrets would be aired. It would not do."

"You're forgetting something," said Toddy. "I'm in no position to make trouble for anyone."

"You mean," Alvarado corrected, "you are in no position to make trouble for yourself. And I am sure you would not. You and I both know that the position of this man is a precarious one. He is, as we noted in an earlier conversation, a sitting duck. You would pick him off, Mr. Kent, even though you did not believe he was the murderer of your wife."

Toddy's eyes fell, and his shoulders drooped. He leaned forward a little, disconsolately, his wrists resting on his knees.

"Do not try it, Mr. Kent."

"You won't shoot," said Toddy. "Someone might hear it."

"Someone might," Alvarado nodded, "but I will shoot if necessary."

"I want to ask a question."

"Quickly, then. And lean back!"

"I know this man didn't kill Elaine. He was with me at the time. But he had her killed, didn't he?"

"He did not. It was the last thing he would have wanted."

"Put it this way. He knew the watch was in our room. He sent someone to get it. Elaine put up a fight, and the guy killed her."

Alvarado shook his head. "This man, with more money than he can spend, would go to such lengths for a watch? . . . And that is two questions you have asked."

"All right, then," Toddy persisted, "she'd found out something about him. She tried to work some blackmail and—"

"She did not," interrupted Alvarado. "Let me repeat, he did not want your wife dead. And now, stand up!"

"All right." Toddy got carefully to his feet. "What about giving the departing guest a drink?"

"Of course." Alvarado did not hesitate for so much as an instant. "The cellarette is there . . . and the carafe is heavy. It would be futile to attempt to throw it."

"I don't intend to," said Toddy, honestly.

"And instead of the large drink, which you doubtless desire, take two very small ones. Not enough, to be explicit, to have any effect if thrown."

Toddy sidled along the lounge to the corner cellarette. His eyes watchful, apprehensive, he turned his back on the chinless man and picked up the carafe.

Toddy tipped the carafe and slopped a fraction of an ounce of brandy into a highball glass. He raised it, holding his breath; but Chinless apparently was also holding his. Either that or he hadn't moved: he was still standing by the desk.

Toddy lowered the glass, his thumb pressing with restrained firmness toward the lip. It gave against the pressure; a little more and it would break. But would it break as it had to—and when it had to? There wouldn't be time to turn. The blow would have to be on its way down. If it wasn't, Alvarado would shoot. He'd have to, and he would.

Toddy set the glass down again, rattling the carafe against it as he poured his second drink. He heard it, then: an almost imperceptible squeak of the floor, all but masked by the sound of the glassware.

He lifted the glass, pressing steadily, harder. Suddenly there was no resistance to his thumb, and he heard the swift uprush of air; and he thrust the broken glass up and back, dropping into a crouch in the same split second.

The glass exploded in his hand. His whole arm went numb. There was a wild curse of pain and the clatter of metal against wood. He whirled, awkward in his crouch, and threw himself at the gun. Alvarado kicked him solidly in the solar plexus. He sprawled, paralyzed, and Alvarado kicked him again. He lay fighting for breath, every nerve screaming with shock.

Alvarado picked up the gun. Cursing frightfully as it

slipped in his grasp, he shifted it to his left hand. He advanced on Toddy, his right hand scarlet, dripping with blood.

"It is bad, eh, Mr. Kent? But do not worry about it. I will bind it up in a minute. A very few minutes. . . . Actually I am grateful for what you did. What was a painful duty now becomes a pleasure."

He grasped Toddy's ankle with the lacerated hand, grimaced painfully, and dragged him toward the hall door. "Do not resist me, Mr. Kent. Make no overt move. If it should mean my instant death, I would not hesitate. . . ."

Toddy didn't try anything. He couldn't. It was still a desperate struggle to get his breath.

"Now . . ." Alvarado opened the door, tugged him through it, panting, and kicked it shut again. "Now—" Alvarado regrasped his ankle, backed and dragged him down the hallway. His eyes glinted insanely. He was incoherent with fury.

"Now, you will see, Mr. Kent. . . . You will be one of the dogs. *Pobre* Perrito's twin, yes. The one the obliging gentleman from the crematory did not see. . . . Dolores was to have served, but it will be all right. The added weight is excusable. It is the practice, the gentleman tells me, to enclose the pet's belongings . . . the bed . . . the eating and drinking receptacles. . . . So many things and such big dogs. . . ."

He opened a second door, tugged furiously, and slammed it shut. And Toddy knew at last the reason for the chinless man's perfume.

The air was heavy with the odor of chloroform. The room with its tightly closed windows swam with its sickening-sweet stench.

Alvarado released his ankle, and Toddy tried to sit up. He fell back, groaning, and his head banged against the wall. He lay there, not quite prone, staring dully at the two long pine boxes on the floor. Alvarado chuckled.

He had wiped his sweating face, and now it and his hand were both scarlet. He was smeared with blood; his face was a hideous, blood-smeared mask.

The mask crinkled in a mirthless grin, and he picked up a hammer from one of the boxes. He hefted it in his hand, gazing steadily at Toddy, inching a little toward him. And then he burst into another laugh.

"Do not worry, Mr. Kent. There is nothing to worry about yet. I would first have you observe something. . . ."

He inserted the claw of the hammer between one of the boxes and its lid. He pried downward, moved the hammer, reinserted the claw and pried again.

"You do not understand, eh?" he panted. "So much effort—so much more, thanks to you. Why not, simply, since I am leaving, leave the bodies here? It is this way"— he wiped, smeared, his face again—"there is always the chance of some flaw in planning; the possibility of apprehension. And murder is regarded much more seriously than smuggling. But even without that, without error or misfortune, there would be great unpleasantness. Your squeamish countrymen would be outraged, your newspapers vocal. In the end, my government might be faced with demands for my person. . . ."

He laid down the hammer and tugged at the lid with his hand. Wincing, he looked carefully at Toddy. He nodded, satisfied with what he saw, and dropped the gun into his pocket. He grasped the lid with both hands, pulled and swung it open on its hinges.

"Now," he said, and started to stoop. "No," he shook his head. "She must lie on the bottom. Otherwise . . ."

Picking up the hammer, he turned to the other box and began unsealing its lid. The gun remained in his pocket, but the fact meant nothing to Toddy. He was breathing more easily, but he still felt paralyzed.

"Evidence . . ." Alvarado was murmuring. "But there will be none, not a particle; only ashes scattered to the winds. . . . Strong suspicions, yes, but no evidence. Nothing to act upon. . . ."

The lid swung free. Alvarado lifted out the girl, held her for a moment, then shrugged and tossed her to the bed. "Still alive, like the dog doubtless. It does not matter. I will prepare another sponge, and it has several hours to work."

He started to turn. Then, catching Toddy's eye, he nodded solemnly.

"You are right, of course. They weigh little, but the weight already is overmuch. They will have to come off."

He jerked off her shoes, and dropped them to the floor. Then the stockings. He grasped the dress at its throat, and ripped it off with one furious tug . . . The brassière, then. And then. . . .

He glanced down critically at the nude, undulant figure, and grinned spitefully at Toddy. "Tempting," he said. "You are incapacitated, unfortunately, but there is no reason why I . . . You could enjoy that, Mr. Kent? You would derive pleasure from mine?"

"Y-you,"—Toddy rasped—"bastard . . ."

"I shall kick you some more," Alvarado promised. "As for Dolores, she shall lie with the dog, poor Perrito. He deserved it, eh, Mr. Kent? It is small recompense for the death which expedience forces me to inflict. . . . If he were smaller, if he could not talk, I might have . . ."

Going down on his knees, he looked regretfully at the dog. He got an arm under it, stroked the head absently with his bleeding hand.

"*Pobre Perrito,*" he murmured. "I am sorry."

A shudder ran through the dog's body. His tongue lolled

out, touched Alvarado's hand. It moved against the hand, licking.

"Cruel," murmured Alvarado. "You are nearly dead, and I let you revive. I let in the air. I kill you twice. . . ."

He got up abruptly, brushing at his eyes, and turned to the bed. He lifted the girl and lowered her roughly into the box from which he had taken her.

"Now," he said, bending over the dog again, "it will soon be over."

This time he put both arms under the great black body, and grunting stood erect with it. The animal's eyes slitted open. The huge jaws gaped lazily. Alvarado bent his head—his scarlet face.

The dog's jaws snapped shut on it.

The blood scent . . . Like a dream, a nightmare, a scene at the Los Angeles house came back to Toddy. . . . *Shake and Donald, their faces spouting blood. And Alvarado holding the lunging dog* . . .

Alvarado was bent over, staggering. His fists flailed against the dog and his muffled, smothered shrieks emerged as a horrible humming . . . *"Hmmmm? Mmm-mmm! MMMMMM! . . ."*

Toddy yelled. He got to his hands and knees and lurched forward, tried to grasp the dog by a leg. How this had come about didn't matter now. He only knew that it had to be stopped.

There was a roar in the room and Toddy dropped to his stomach. Alvarado had got out his gun, but he couldn't aim it. He was pivoting in a slow, pain-crazed waltz; doubled over, the automatic sweeping the walls. And the dog waltzed with him, eyes closed, jaws clamped, its hind claws rattling and scratching against the floor.

Suddenly, Alvarado's right arm shot straight out from

his body. The dog moved—they moved together—and the gun swerved. It steadied, pointing at the girl.

Toddy could never say how he did it; he could never recall doing it. But somehow he was on his feet, his hands gripping a bony scarlet wrist. He threw his weight forward, and there was a long staccato roar—that and the shattering of glass as the windowpane behind a drawn curtain was blown into bits.

Then, somewhere, in the not too distant distance, a motor raced and an automobile horn tooted angrily.

Toddy staggered backward and sat down on the bed.

Alvarado and the dog lay on the floor, motionless. One paw rested against Alvarado's shoulder, and Alvarado's left hand lay on the dog's black hide. The dog had released his hold at last. What the jaws had clung to was no longer there.

Toddy bent forward suddenly and retched. His dizziness disappeared and he could think again.

He'd have to get out of here—he gripped the edge of the bedstead and pulled himself upright. Those shots had made a hell of a racket; it sounded like they might have grazed a car. It might take the cops a little while to discover their source, but when they did . . . Well, they wouldn't find him here. Alvarado had dough on him. Plenty of it. And the keys to the convertible were in the switch. By the time the cops got a line on him, he'd be through Tijuana, heading for one of the fishing villages below Rosarita Beach. From there, for a price, he could get passage to Central America.

Of course, he'd be on the run for the rest of his life. He'd always have Elaine's murder hanging over him. That couldn't be helped. When you couldn't fight you had to run.

He got up. Eyes averted, he was bending over Alvarado's body, starting to search for the money that must be there, when something made him pause. He straightened, shrugged irritatedly, and stooped again. He stood up again, cursing.

He picked up the girl and laid her on the bed. His tanned face flushed, he pulled one side of the spread over her.

That was all he could do. He wasn't any doctor. Anyway, she'd be all right. She . . .

He pressed his thumb and forefinger against her wrist.

At first there seemed to be no pulse. Then he felt it, faint, stuttering, strengthening for a few beats, then fading again.

His voice trailed off into silence. Angry, desperate. Someone might not be there. Not soon enough. They might— but they might not. She was right on the edge. A little longer and she might be over it.

He dropped her hand—almost flung it from him—and raced into the front room. His shoes grated against the broken glass, as he snatched up the brandy carafe. He let it slide from his fingers, fall gurgling to the floor.

He knew better than that, after all the talks he'd had with Elaine's doctors. Alcohol wasn't a stimulant but a depressant. An anesthetic. Taken on top of the chloroform it would mean certain death.

Running to the kitchen, he yanked open the cupboard doors. No ammonia. Nothing that would act as a restorative.

He glanced at the stove. A coffee pot stood on the back burner. It was half full.

As soon as the coffee began to simmer, he grabbed the pot and a cup and hurried back to the bedroom. He got down on his knees at the bedside, filled a cup and set the pot on the floor, and raised the girl's head.

Her head wobbled and coffee ran from her lips, down over her chin and neck.

He put an arm around her, under her left arm, and rested her head on his shoulder. He poured more coffee in the cup.

This time she swallowed some of the liquid, but a shuddering, strangled gasp made him suddenly jerk the cup away. Too fast—he'd given it to her too fast. She'd smother, drown actually, if he wasn't careful.

He waited a minute—an hour it seemed like—and again placed the cup to her lips. Mentally, he measured out a spoonful, and waited until her throat moved, swallowed. He gave her another spoonful, then waited, and another swallow.

Slowly, a little color was returning to her face. Maybe it would be all right now if he . . . He felt her pulse. Sighing, he refilled the cup.

He had almost finished doling it out to her, a spoonful at a time, when her heart began to pound. He could feel it against his hand, skipping a little, still a little irregular, but going stronger with every beat.

He started to remove his hand, but her arm had tightened against her side. Her eyelids fluttered drowsily, and opened.

"You're all—" he began.

"You . . . all right . . . Toddy . . . ?"

"Yeah, sure," he said, somehow shamed. "Now, look, I've got to beat it. Alvarado's dead. The cops'll be here any minute. I—"

"They do not know about . . ."

"They'll find out!" Toddy didn't know why he was arguing. He didn't know why the hell he didn't just beat it. "Anyway, there's plenty without that. I'm wanted in half a dozen—half a dozen—"

Her arm had gone around his neck. Her other arm held his hand against her breast. The beat of her heart was very firm now. Firm and fast.

"I tell you, I've got to—"

Her lips shut off the words. She sank back against the pillows, drawing him with her.

. . . Faintly, then louder and louder, a police siren moaned and whined. Toddy didn't hear it.

22

In the early afternoon of his third day in jail, he sat in semi-isolation in a corner of the bullpen, mulling over his situation.

He knew he was being held at the instance of the federal authorities. Which meant that, since a murder charge would take precedence over others, Elaine's death hadn't been discovered. That seemed impossible; Alvarado himself had seen detectives in his and Elaine's hotel room. But the fact remained. He wasn't—couldn't be—wanted for murder. Yet.

He also knew that Milt Vonderheim was the smuggling ring's gold-supplier, and, more than likely, the man who had had Elaine killed. Why the last, he didn't know; but the first was indisputable. It was no wonder that Milt had wanted him disposed of quickly. Since Toddy's original visit to the house of the talking dog, he had held most of the clues to the little jeweler's real identity.

He had presented Milt's card that day and mentioned being sent by a friend. And Alvarado, not knowing what might be in the air, had admitted him. He had discovered almost immediately, of course, that Toddy knew nothing of Milt's illegal activities—that he had simply stumbled onto the house. But Alvarado had been prepared for that eventuality. . . . His eyes were "bad." He hadn't been able to read the card. In other words, Toddy's entry had not been obtained through Milt.

It was a shrewd subterfuge, but it had one great weakness. It could only be explained, if explanation became necessary, on one basis. Milt was the ring's key man: the gold-supplier. Since he was operating in the open and was confined to his shop, he could handle no other end of the racket.

Toddy's fingers strayed absently to the shirt pocket of his jail khakis, and came away empty. No cigarettes. No dough. And he'd hardly been able to touch the jail chow except for the coffee. The lack of comforts, however, troubled him much less than the reason for the lack. He'd never been able to do time. He couldn't now. And he was going to have to do a lot unless—

They'd have his record by now. They'd know where he was wanted and for how much. Sixty days. Ninety. A hundred and ten. Six months. A year and a . . . And Elaine. Why think about those other raps when they were certain to pin a murder on him?

He tried to accept that fact and salvage what he could from it. He'd killed her, say, but not with premeditation. She'd slugged him with a bottle, and he'd blanked out and killed her. Not intentionally. In a fit of temper. That was manslaughter; second degree manslaughter, if he had the right lawyer. If he was lucky, he'd get off with five years.

He thought about that, those five years. He thought about Dolores, then thrust her firmly out of his mind. Jail was hard enough to take without thinking about her, knowing that she'd come into his life too late, that never again . . . never again . . .

All day long an oval of men circled the bullpen, moving around and around in silent restlessness. When one man dropped out, another took his place in the oval. Its composition changed a hundred times, and yet it itself never changed.

"Kent!"

The oval stopped moving. Every eye was on the door.

"Todd Kent! Front and center!"

Toddy got up, dusted off the seat of his trousers, and pushed his way through the other prisoners.

Clint McKinley, bureau chief of investigation for the Treasury Department, was a stocky mild-looking man with thin red hair and a soft, amiable voice. He wasn't a great deal older than Toddy, and, in his first brief sizing up, Toddy decided that he wasn't too sharp a character. He wasn't long in revising that opinion.

McKinley seated him in a chair in front of his desk, tossed him a package of cigarettes, and even held a match for him. Then he folded his hands, leaned his elbows on the desk, stared straight at Toddy and began to talk. About Dolores, or, as he called her, Miss Chavez.

"We have a lot of admiration for her," he said. "She did the right thing at great personal risk and without hope of reward. We're going to do the right thing by her. She's in this country on a student's visa. We're going to pave the way for her to become a citizen. We're going to do everything else that's in our power to do. That can be quite a lot."

Toddy nodded. "I'm glad for her. She's a nice girl."

"Now we come to you," said McKinley. "We've gone into your record pretty thoroughly. We find it remarkable. You've preyed on your fellow citizens with one kind of racket or another ever since you went into circulation. You get a chance in the Army to redeem yourself, and you throw it away. You sell out. You help to tear down the prestige of the flag you swore allegiance to. You've never been any good. You've never done a single unselfish, honest deed in your whole life."

The soft, amiable voice ceased to speak. Toddy pushed himself up from his chair. "Thanks for the sermon," he said. "I don't think I'll stay for the singing."

"Sit down, Kent."

"Huh-uh. You people can't make a charge stick against me. You've had no right to hold me this long."

"We can see that you're held by other authorities."

"Hop to it, then."

"What's the hurry?" said McKinley. "It always gets me to see a man throw himself away. Maybe I said a little too much. If I did, I'll apologize."

Toddy sat back down. He had intended to from the beginning. It had simply seemed bad, psychologically, to let McKinley crack the whip too hard.

"As a matter of fact," McKinley continued, "I think my statement was a little sweeping. If you hadn't tried to help Miss Chavez there in San Diego, you might have escaped. That's something in your favor. Of course, you may have had some selfish motive for staying. But—"

"Try real hard," said Toddy. "You'll think of one."

"Don't coax me." McKinley's eyes glinted. "You want to get along with me or not, Kent? If you don't, just say so. I've got something better to do with my time than argue with two-bit con men."

Toddy swallowed harshly and got a grip on himself. He'd been kidding himself about that psychology business. A little, anyway. He was losing his temper. He was letting a cop get his goat.

"You're trying to do a job," he said, "but you're going about it the wrong way. You're not softening me up. You're getting nowhere fast. Now why don't you drop it and start all over again?"

"Who supplied the gold to this outfit, Kent?"

"I don't know."

"You've got a good idea."

"Maybe."

"Let's have it, then. Come on. Spit it out."

"No," said Toddy.

"You want a deal, huh? All right. You play square with me, and I'll do what I can for you."

"That," said Toddy, "isn't my idea of a deal."

"I'll give you one more chance, Kent. I don't believe you know anything, anyway, but I'm willing to give you a chance. Turn it down and you'll be touring jails for the next three years."

Toddy grinned derisively. *Three years, hell!* McKinley misunderstood the grin. He jabbed a button on his desk, and the deputy jailer came back in.

"Take him out of here," said McKinley. "Lock him up and throw the key away. We won't want him anymore."

The jailer took Toddy's elbow. Toddy got up and they started for the door. He was sick inside. He'd played his cards the only way he could, but they just hadn't been good enough. Now it was all over.

"Kent."

The jailer paused, gave Toddy a nudge. Toddy didn't turn around. He didn't say anything. He was afraid to.

"This is your last chance, Kent. You go through that door and you'll never get another one."

Toddy hesitated, shrugged. He took a step toward the door and his hand closed over the knob. He turned it. Behind him he heard McKinley's amiable, unwilling chuckle.

"All right. Come on back. I'll talk to Kent a little longer, Chief."

The jailer went out the door. Toddy, the palms of his hands damp, went back to his chair.

"All right," said McKinley calmly, as though the scene just past had never taken place. "You were saying I was going about my job the wrong way. Could be. I've been in this work for fifteen years, but I learn something new every day. Now tell me where you think I was wrong."

"You want something definite from me," said Toddy. "You haven't offered anything definite in return."

"We can't actually promise anything. Except to use our influence."

"That's good enough for me."

"Call it settled, then. We'll try to wipe the slate clean." McKinley smiled. "You haven't committed any murders anywhere, have you? I don't think we could square those."

Toddy shook his head. "No murders."

"Good," said McKinley. "Now, let's see what we've got. You were buying gold. You accidentally—accidentally on purpose, maybe—picked up a valuable watch—a chunk of bullion—at Alvarado's house. He checked on you, found out you were hot, and offered you a job. If you turned it down, he threatened to—"

McKinley broke off and made a deprecating gesture. "Maybe," he said, "Miss Chavez doesn't have her facts straight. Maybe you'd better do the talking."

"She has them straight," said Toddy.

"Why did you go to Tijuana, Kent?"

"Alvarado told me to. I"—Toddy coughed—"I was to go there and wait for him. He didn't say why."

"Cough a little longer," McKinley suggested. "Maybe you can think of a better one."

"No," said Toddy. "I think we'd better let that one stand. There's something in the rules about impeaching your own witnesses. If I *did* take a little gold across the border, it's just as well that you have no knowledge of it."

"Mmmm," drawled McKinley. "You don't know why he wanted you to go there—you weren't in any position to ask questions. So you went, and you got slugged. And if Alvarado hadn't intervened you'd have been killed."

"That's right. It's this way," said Toddy. "After it was all over, Alvarado told me why he'd wanted me to go to Tijuana. He had it in for the gold-supplier. He was trying to wash him up. So Alvarado let him know I was going to this place in Tijuana, hoping that he'd try to kill me."

He paused, conscious of the pitfall he was approaching. How to tell a plausible story without mentioning Elaine.

"Did you ever try telling the truth?" said McKinley. "The complete truth? You might enjoy it."

"I am trying to." Toddy frowned earnestly. "But it's a pretty mixed-up deal. It's hard to explain something when you don't completely understand it yourself. You see, Alvarado wanted to get this guy but he got orders to leave him alone. So he had to back up. He wouldn't tell me anything. I had to guess why I was slugged."

"You knew who the gold-supplier was, in other words?"

"He thought I did—or could find out; it was the only reason he could have for wanting to kill me."

McKinley ran a stubby hand through his thin red hair. He sighed, stood up, and turned to the window. He stared down into the street, hands thrust into his pants pockets, teetering back and forth on his heels.

"It doesn't figure," he said to the window. "It doesn't because you're holding out something. I don't know why, but I'm reasonably sure of one thing. You know who the gold-supplier is."

"I think I know."

"You thought in the beginning. Then you found out. Something Alvarado did or said—something you saw there in the San Diego house—tipped you off." McKinley sat down again and placed his elbows back on the desk.

"Knowing and proving are two different things. Suppose I gave you his name and address. You go there. You don't find anything. He won't talk. . . ."

"That's our problem."

"Is that a promise? Regardless of whether my tip works out, you'll get me that clean slate?"

"Oh, well, now,"—McKinley spread his hands—"you can't expect me to do that. You might give us any old name and address and—and—yeah," said McKinley. "Mmm-hmmm."

He squirmed in his chair, looking down at some papers on his desk. Fumbling with them absently. Abruptly he looked up. "It's Milt Vonderheim! Don't lie! I've got the proof!"

Toddy laughed. After a moment, McKinley grinned.

"It's a good thing you didn't tell me it was Vonderheim. I'd have known you were trying to throw a curve under me."

"I'd pick a better goat than Milt," Toddy said. "Everyone knows that—"

"We know. I don't care about everyone. How would you go about landing this man, Kent?"

"Nothing's been in the papers about Alvarado or—?"

"Nothing yet. I don't know how long we can keep it quiet."

"I'll need a few things. A gun, some money, a car. I'll need a few days. I've got to see some people."

"Why?"

"To make sure," said Toddy, evenly, "that you don't have a tail on me. At the first sign of one, the whole deal's off."

"Why? If you're on the square."

Toddy explained. He was plausible, earnest, the soul of sincerity. If McKinley wouldn't believe this, he thought, he wouldn't believe anything.

"That's the way I'll handle it," he concluded. "He'll have a lot of dough. I'll go through the motions of taking it, highjacking him. Then I'll put him in the car and head for the country. Someplace, supposedly, where I can bump him off and hide his body."

"That part I don't get. Why would you want to bump him off?"

"Because that's the way I'd have to feel about him. When a man's killed"—Toddy caught himself—"when a man's tried to kill you, you want to get back at him. He'll talk. He'll spill everything he knows in attempting to get off the hook."

"Yeah. Maybe," said McKinley.

"But I've got to be left alone. No tails. Nothing that might possibly lead him to think I was working with you. . . . You see that, don't you? It's got to look like I'm giving you the double-cross. Otherwise, he won't talk and you'll never find out how he manages to get pounds of gold every week—you won't be able to prove that he has got it. And if you can't prove that—"

"But suppose," said McKinley. "Suppose you *are* giving us the double-cross?"

Toddy shrugged and leaned back in his chair. McKinley sat blinking, staring at him.

"I'd be crazy to do it," he said, at last. "I give you a car and a gun and a clear field with a man that's loaded with dough. I give a guy like you a setup like that. It doesn't make sense any way you look at it."

He pressed a button on his desk and stood up. Toddy stood up also. It was all over. There was no use arguing.

"Only fifteen years in this game and I've gone crazy," said McKinley. "Chief, take this man back to jail and dress him out. I'll send over an order for his release."

He said one other thing as Toddy headed for the door. Something that made Toddy very glad his back was turned: "We'll spring your wife, too, Kent, as soon as you pull this off. . . ."

23

After visiting a barber shop, Toddy went to a pawnshop—where he purchased a second-hand suitcase—a drugstore, a haberdashery, and a newsstand which sold back issues. Then he checked in at a hotel.

With deliberate slowness he unpacked the suitcase, the clean shirts, socks and underwear, the toilet articles, cigarettes and bottle of whiskey. He knew what the back-issue newspapers would tell him. He had seen an evening paper headline, BAIL RACKET PROBE LOOMS, but without that he would have known. Miracles didn't happen. Elaine couldn't be in jail.

Still, he didn't really *know*, until he read the papers . . . He spread them out at last, a drink in his hand, and read. The foolishly unreasonable hope collapsed.

Only two of the papers carried the story; one gave it a paragraph, the other two. The latter paper also carried her picture, a small, blurred shot, taken several years ago. The former "character actress" had surrendered at a suburban jail. She'd worn sunglasses and was "apparently suffering from a severe cold." Somebody was filling in for Elaine.

Toddy sighed and poured himself another drink. It was about as he'd figured it.

He ordered dinner and put in a call to Airedale. The bondsman arrived just as the waiter was departing.

His derby hat was pulled low over his eyes, and his doggish face was long with anxiety. His first act was to step to the window and draw the shade.

"Can't you smell that stuff, man?" he rasped. "That's gas. It's driftin' all the way down from that little room in Sacramento!"

Toddy poured a glass of milk, handed it to him, and gestured to the bed. Airedale sat down, heavily, fanning himself with the derby.

"Where'd you go," he said. "And why ain't you still goin'?"

"Save it," said Toddy, taking a bite of steak. "Now tell me what happened."

"Me? I tell *you* what happened?"

"They cracked down on your connections. You had to produce Elaine. Take it from there."

"I go to your hotel and get ahold of lardass. We go up to your room. We can't raise no one, so we break in. You ain't there, Elaine ain't there. Period."

"Comma," said Toddy. "How'd the room look? I mean was it torn up?"

"You ought to know. . . . No," Airedale added hastily, "it wasn't."

"There weren't any cops around? No detectives?"

"Just me and the house dick, but—"

"What time were you there?"

"Eleven-thirty, maybe twelve."

"Oh," said Toddy, "I get it. You were there when . . ."

"When," Airedale nodded. "When Elaine was going up in smoke. Jesus, Toddy, did you have to draw a picture of it? Couldn't you have done it outside somewheres? You're up there raising hell—everyone in the joint hears her screamin'—and then—"

"That doesn't mean anything. She was always doing that."

"She won't anymore," said Airedale. "I honest to Gawd

don't get it, Toddy. Getting rid of the corpus delicti won't make you nothing. Not with that incinerator stack running right through your room."

Toddy abruptly pushed aside his steak and poured a cup of coffee. "I didn't kill her, Airedale. Let's get that straight. I didn't kill her."

"Am I a cop?" said Airedale. "I don't care what you did. I ain't even seen you. I ain't even telling you to get away from here as far and as fast as you can before they put the arm on you."

"There hasn't been any rumble yet."

"There will be," Airedale assured him grimly. "It's building up right now. That little hustler, the ringer that's standing in for Elaine, don't like jail."

"So?" Toddy shrugged. "She's in up to her ears. It would be easier for her if she liked it."

"She don't like it," Airedale repeated, "because she's on the dope. She's a heroin mainliner."

Toddy gulped. "But why in the hell did she—"

"Why do they do anything when they're hitting the *H*?" growled Airedale. "She spent so much time in the hay she was starting to moo, but she still couldn't pay for her habit. So she stands in for Elaine, and then she gives me the bad news. I'm over a barrel, see? I've got to take care of her. I got to put in a fix and see that she gets the stuff. Either that or I'm out of business. She'll squawk that she ain't Elaine."

Airedale paused to light a cigar. He took a disconsolate puff or two, and sat staring at the glowing tip.

"Well . . . I've had a doctor in every day. Cold shots, y'know. But that can't go on more'n a few more trips. Even if no one wised up and I was getting those shots for a buck instead of a hundred, I'd have to break it off. I wouldn't play. I've got my own kind of crookedness. It don't drive people crazy. It don't kill 'em."

He paused again, and gave Toddy an apologetic glance. "Not," he said, "that some of 'em don't need killin'. It's just a manner of speaking."

"Skip it," said Toddy. "Will she keep quiet as long as she gets the stuff?"

"Why not? She ain't a bad kid. She doesn't want to cause any trouble. She's beginning to see that I can't keep her fixed, and she ain't kickin'. She'll just go out on her own again."

"She won't be able to do that. They'll stick her on a con-spiracy charge."

"Huh-uh." Airedale wagged his head. "She'll get out. She'll get all the stuff she wants. You've read them papers? Well, that little gal's worth her weight in white stuff to cer-tain parties."

The bondsman stubbed out his cigar, sighed, and reached inside the pocket of his coat. He brought out a railroad timetable and proceeded to scan it. After a mo-ment, he looked up.

"What do you think about Florida this time of year?"

"I'm not going anywhere," said Toddy. "Not yet, any-way."

"I am," said Airedale. "I like my fireworks on the Fourth of July. Here's hoping it'll be safe to come back by then."

He waited, as though expecting some comment, but Toddy only nodded. Naturally, Airedale would have to get out of town. The scandal would die down, eventually, be superseded by other and livelier scandals. Meanwhile, Los Angeles would be made extremely uncomfortable for the bondsman and his various political connections.

Airedale rose, looked into the crown of his derby, and emitted a bark of pleasure. "Well, look at that," he said, pulling forth a roll of bills. "And just when you'd changed your mind about leaving!"

"Thanks." Toddy pushed back the roll. "It isn't that. I've got money."

"So? What else do you need?"

"Nothing you can help me with."

"I can help you a little," said Airedale. "I can tell you to forget it if you're figuring on copping a plea. Juries don't like these cases where the body is disposed of. It shows bad faith, see what I mean? You try to cover the crime up and then, maybe, when you see you can't get away with it, you ask for a break. They give you one. Up here."

"But—Yeah," said Toddy, dully, "I suppose you're right."

Airedale slammed on his derby and started to turn away. "I don't get it," he snarled. "What are you hanging around for? Why ain't you on your way?"

"I want to find out who killed Elaine."

"Brother," said Airedale, "that does it!"

"If I run," said Toddy, "I've got to keep running. A few hundred or a few grand won't be enough. I've got to be squared for life."

"You've got something good lined up, huh?" said Airedale. "Why didn't you say so in the first place? What—never mind. Can you pull it off by yourself?"

"It's the only way I can do it. But I'll need more time, Airedale. A couple of days, anyway. I really wanted three, but—"

"Two," said Airedale. "I'd figured on twenty-four hours—enough time for me to clear out. But I'll fix the gal for two; I'll pay for that much. She may not get the stuff if I'm not here, but . . . Oh, hell. I guess it'll be all right."

They shook hands and Airedale left. A drink in his hand, Toddy sat down on the bed and mulled over the situation. Some of his normal fatalism began to assert itself. He grinned philosophically.

He undressed and climbed into bed. Lying back with his eyes open, he stared up into the darkness.

McKinley had promised not to have him tailed. It wouldn't be necessary. Placed at strategic points, a mere handful of men, with the license number and description of a car, could follow its movements even in a city as large as Los Angeles. So there was only one thing to do—rather, two things. Change the license, change the description.

Milt would be stubborn. He'd do nothing unless he was made to—so he'd be made to. There'd be no spot-check, no tails, no T-men to interfere.

24

At nine-thirty the next morning, Toddy finished a leisurely breakfast in his room and called McKinley. The bureau chief sounded annoyed as he told Toddy where to pick up the car.

"You haven't seen Miss Chavez?" he asked.

"Seen her? Why the hell would I? I don't even know where—"

"Good," said McKinley, in a milder tone. "She's been after us to find out what happened to you. Wanted to see you in jail. Wanted to send you a note. I finally told her we'd turned you loose, and you'd left town."

"That's—that's fine," said Toddy.

"Yeah. You've got a job to do, Kent. You've got a wife. And Miss Chavez is as straight as they come."

"And I'm not."

"You're not," agreed McKinley. "You took the words right out of my mouth."

He hung up the phone. Toddy slammed up his receiver, and finished dressing.

He was irritated by the conversation, but more than that, worried. Dolores knew about Elaine's death. She'd be wondering why, after holding him, Toddy, three days, McKinley had suddenly freed him. She'd be sure that instead of merely leaving town, as McKinley had told her he had, he'd try to leave the country. She'd know that he'd need plenty of money to leave on and that he could only get it in one way.

As long as he was in jail, her deal with the government was safe. They wouldn't care, when the news of the murder broke, whether she'd known about it or not. But if he skipped the country and committed another crime in the process of skipping . . .

No—Toddy shook his head. That wasn't like her. She wouldn't be concerned for herself, but him. She'd want to help him. And that, in a way, was as bad as the other. He couldn't tell her anything. This had to be a one-man show.

Toddy took a final glance around the room, left it, and headed for the elevator.

The car was parked a few blocks away. He almost laughed aloud when he saw it. It was a medium-priced sedan, exactly like thousands of others of the same make to a casual observer. But Toddy was not observing casually, and neither would the T-men.

They'd hardly need to look at the license plates. The gray paint job, the white sidewall tires and the red-glass reflector buttons by which the plates were held would be sufficient identification. They'd be able to spot him two blocks away.

He slid under the wheel, and opened the dashboard compartment. The keys and the gun were there, and—he checked it quickly—the gun was loaded. Everything was as it should be.

He drove north and east, winding back and forth through a maze of side streets, avoiding anything in the nature of an arterial thoroughfare. He didn't think McKinley would have his spot check set up so soon, but he might; and there wasn't any hurry. He had the whole day to kill.

The houses he passed grew shabbier, fewer and farther apart. Many of them stood empty. Most of the streets were unpaved. It was one of those borderline, ambiguous areas common to most cities; an area surrendered to industry but not yet made part of it.

Toddy pulled onto a brick-paved street, and rounded a corner. On the opposite side of the street was an abandoned warehouse. On the right, the side he was on, was an automobile salvage yard, its high board fence set back to allow room for the dingy filling station at the front. A four-wheel truck trailer, all its tires missing, stood between the street and the closed-in grease rack.

Toddy drove into the inside lane of the station. He spoke a few words to a cold-eyed man in greasy coveralls and a skullcap made of an old hat. The man leaned against the gas pump. He looked up and down the street, said "Okay, Mac," and jerked his head. Toddy drove into the greasing tunnel; then, as the rear wall slid up, into the yard beyond.

The job took two men three hours. When it was over Toddy himself, if he had not watched the transformation, would not have believed it was the same car.

A chromium grille disguised the radiator. The white sidewalls were replaced with plain tires. A sunshade sheltered the windshield. The roof and fenders of the car were dark blue; the rest of the body a glossy black. The red reflector buttons were gone, of course, as were the original license plates. The plate holders, with the substitute plates, had been moved to a new position.

Toddy paid over one hundred and fifty dollars, adding a five-dollar tip for each of the workmen. That left him with a little less than ten dollars, but that was more than enough for what he had to do. He wouldn't be paying his hotel bill. He wouldn't be going back to pay it.

He took one of the main streets back toward town, stopping once at a restaurant-bar, where he passed the better part of two hours, and again at a drugstore where he bought faintly tinted sunglasses. The glasses were disguise enough; not really necessary, for that matter. They'd be looking for a car, not a man.

It was dusk when Toddy reached the city's business section, and a light drizzling rain was beginning to fall. Driving slowly, Toddy turned north up Spring Street.

Milt wouldn't be buying gold, now. Moreover, he wouldn't be receiving his nightly visit from the driver of the beer truck. He wouldn't because there would be no more scrap gold to go out in the empty bottles.

Toddy swore suddenly and stepped on the gas. Almost immediately, he slowed down again. So what? What difference did it make if he passed by the hotel, the one where he and Elaine had lived? They didn't know anything or want to know anything. All they were interested in was the rent which was paid through tomorrow.

He parked on Main Street, and sat in the growing darkness, smoking, listening to the patter of rain on the roof. For a panic-stricken moment he wondered whether Milt had already skipped; then grinned and shook his head. Milt would see no need to hurry. He'd move cautiously, safely, taking his time.

So that was all right. He wished he had nothing to worry about but that.

It was seven o'clock by the time he had finished his third cigarette. He tossed the butt out the window, transferred the gun from the dash compartment to his pocket, and started the car.

He drove up Main a block, swung over to the next street, drove back three blocks. On a dark side street he turned right and cut the motor. He coasted to a stop a few doors above the entrance to the Los Angeles Watch & Jewelry Co., brokers in precious metals.

Luckily, he waited a moment before reaching for the

door of the car. For Milt hadn't stopped buying gold. Doubtless he felt that it was too soon, that he had to go through the motions a little longer. Or perhaps he was waiting for a weekend to beat it. At any rate, the door of the shop opened suddenly and a raincoated figure carrying the familiar square box dashed toward Main Street. A few minutes later, two other buyers came out together and trotted toward Main.

Crouched low in the seat, hidden by the rain-washed windows, Toddy waited ten minutes more. But no one else emerged from the shop, and, he decided, no one was likely to. It was too late.

He slid over on the seat and rolled down the window. He looked swiftly up and down the street. Then he rolled up the window, opened the door, and got out.

He walked close to the building fronts, pausing as he passed the one next to Milt's shop. He could see in from there—see a scene so familiar, so associated with warmth and friendliness, that what he was about to do seemed suddenly fantastic and hateful.

Milt, seated back in his cage, the bright work light lifting him out of the shadows, draping him in a kind of golden aura. Milt . . . how could he . . . ?

But he had. And his friendliness—his faked friendship—only made matters worse. Toddy reconnoitered the street quickly, strode to the door, and stepped inside. He was halfway down the long dark aisle before Milt could look up.

"Toddy! Iss it you? For days I have been worrying about . . . about . . ."

"Yeah," said Toddy. "I'll bet you have."

He moved swiftly through the wicket of the cage, and brought a hand down on the gooseneck of the lamp. It flattened against the workbench, casting its light upon the floor. No one looking in from the street would see anything.

Milt had started to rise, but Toddy shoved him back in his chair. He seated himself, facing the little jeweler.

"That's right," he nodded grimly. "That's a gun. If you don't think I'll use it, give me a little trouble."

"But I do not understand! Trouble? Have ever I—" He broke off, staring into Toddy's cold set face, and abruptly his mask of bewildered innocence vanished. "Stupid Toddy. Oh, so stupid. At last he awakens."

"Get it out," said Toddy. "Every goddamned nickel. And don't ask me what."

"Ask?" Milt shrugged. "I am not given to foolish chatter. As for *it*, I have anticipated you. It is already out." He started to reach beneath the workbench, then paused abruptly, arm half-extended.

Toddy nodded. "Go ahead. Just don't try anything."

He took the heavy briefcase that Milt drew out, laid it on the bench, and slipped the catch. He shook it slightly, his eyes swerving from the jeweler to the bench. There was one packet of scat money—fives, tens and twenties. The rest of the horde was in thousand-dollar bills, dough too hot for the dumbest burglar to touch. Milt couldn't spend it in this country. Abroad, there'd be no trouble. Violation of income tax laws was not an extraditable offense.

"Your visit was most inopportune," sighed Milt. "A few hours more and I would have been gone."

"You're still going. You're going out to Venice with me, out to the beach. We're going to have a nice long talk."

"We can do that here. We are alone on this street. No one will come in."

"Someone will tomorrow."

"But . . . Oh," said Milt. "Still, is it necessary, Toddy?

You have the money. By tomorrow, you can be very far away. In any case, my hands are tied. I dare not complain."

Toddy jerked his head. "I'll be a lot farther away the day after tomorrow. And you'd talk, all right. Everyone that's had anything to do with me will get a going-over. I've been in jail, and—"

"Yes. I know."

"Then you probably know how I got myself sprung. You know I can't keep my bargain unless I dig up the guy that killed Elaine."

"Which you cannot do," said Milt. "Not"—he added—"that you have any intention of keeping your bargain. Another, perhaps, almost any other man, but not you." He grinned faintly, his hands clasped over his fat stomach. "You do not want to keep your bargain with the government agents. You cannot keep it. A confession you may extract from me, but it will be worthless. I can prove that I did not kill Elaine or cause her to be killed."

"Maybe." Toddy studied the bland, chubby face. "Maybe," he repeated, "but I'm taking you with me, anyway. No one knows how you worked this setup here. I'm going to find out, just in case I ever get back to this country. If you come clean with me I may just tie you up and dump you somewhere. Some place where you'll be found in a few days. Otherwise . . ."

He gestured significantly with the gun. Milt laughed openly.

"Yes? You were thinking of the dunes, doubtless? Oh, excellent! It will be a wonderful place to leave a body . . . or should I say two?"

"Two?" Toddy frowned. "What the hell are you talking about?"

"Bodies," said Milt. "Yours and Miss Chavez'."

Toddy's chair grated against the floor. "Damn you! If you've hurt that—"

Behind him the curtains rustled faintly. Something cold and hard pushed through them, pressed into the back of his neck.

Milt nodded to him, solemnly. "That is right, Toddy. Sit still. Sit very, very still. Yes, and I think I shall just take your gun. Miss Chavez"—he glanced at the clock—"should be here at any moment. Your hotel, your former hotel, I should say, was kind enough to refer her to me. I suggested that she return here tonight when you, in your hour of dire emergency, would most certainly come to me for aid. So . . . So"—the front door opened and clicked softly shut—"she has come."

She came down the aisle, hesitantly at first, then with quick firm steps as she saw the two men in the dim glow of the lamp. "Toddy! I am so glad I—I—"

"Do not scream," said Milt. "Do not move."

He thrust himself up from his chair, moved around Toddy and out through the wicket. Toddy waited helplessly, his hands carefully held out from his sides. . . . This was the one thing he hadn't foreseen—the fact that Milt might have a confederate. Who the hell could it be, he wondered, and why had Milt behaved as he had? What had he hoped to gain by appearing defenseless, letting Toddy talk?

Toddy didn't know, and there was no time now to think about it. The person behind him came through the drapes, and the gun barrel dug viciously into his neck.

He got up slowly. He looked into Dolores' pale strained face, and tried to grin reassuringly. He heard Milt's chuckle as he pushed her forward through the wicket.

He turned around.

"Hi-ya, prince," said Elaine.

25

Through a blinding downpour of rain, the car moved cautiously, steadily westward. Toddy drove, bent over the wheel, staring through the windshield. Dolores was at his side, Milt and Elaine in the rear seat. It was almost an hour before the city proper was left behind them, and silently, except for the humming of the tires and the wet lash of the windshield wipers, they went rolling down Olympic Boulevard. It ran in practically a straight line to the ocean. There was almost no traffic on it now.

Toddy eased up on the gas a little more. He'd outsmarted himself this time. In outwitting McKinley, he'd handed Milt a setup. Now there was nothing to do but stall, postpone the inevitable as long as possible.

The air was thick with the odor of Elaine's cigarettes and whiskey. She coughed, choked, and a fine spray showered Toddy's neck. Milt cleared his throat, apologetically.

"Perhaps, *Liebling,* it might be well to . . ."

"What?" said Elaine. "You trying to tell me when to take a drink?"

Milt hesitated. Toddy felt a faint surge of hope. If she and Milt should start fighting, if she'd only throw one of those wild tantrums of hers . . . But she didn't. Moreover, Toddy knew, she wasn't going to.

"If you put it that way," Milt said, coldly, "yes. Rather, I am telling you when not to drink. And I am telling you that now. There is too much at stake. Later it will be all right; I would be the last to interfere."

There was a moment of silence. Then, "All right,

honey," Elaine said meekly. "You just tell li'l Elaine what to do and that's what she'll do."

"Good," said Milt complacently. "We must give our Toddy no advantage, *hein?*"

"Whatever you say, honey."

"He is a very intelligent man," Milt went on. "He tells me in substance how much time the police have given him. He informs me, indirectly, that there is no one following his movements. Finally, by a reverse process, he makes excellent suggestions for disposing of himself. Do you wonder that I fear him, this intellectual giant?"

Elaine's giggle tapered off to a troubled note. "Yeah, but honey. I don't—"

"Consider," Milt continued, enjoyably. "Everything he is told, yet nothing he sees. He knows that Alvarado has told the anonymous gold-supplier of the theft of the watch. He knows his wife detests him, and he is thoroughly familiar with her talents as an actress. But does he draw any conclusions from these things? Not at all. He is baffled by her strange death and the subsequent disappearance of her body. It does not occur to him that she had simulated death, that she followed him down the fire escape taking the watch with her."

Dolores half-turned in the seat and her eyes flashed. "He is not stupid! He trusted you! It is easy to—"

"Of stupidity," said Milt, "you are hardly a competent judge. You who revealed his release from jail to a stranger. Now if you wish to take full advantage of your remaining minutes of consciousness, you will turn around."

"You are too cowardly! I—"

"Turn around," said Toddy softly. "She called the turn on you, Milt. I trusted you. On top of that, you had a lot of luck. If I hadn't chased off after Donald, I'd have found out that Elaine was pulling a fake."

"There was no element of luck," Milt said. "I telephoned Elaine when you left the shop. There was ample time to locate the watch and prepare for your arrival."

"But if I'd examined Elaine . . ."

"If you had—well, it would be a prank; and later we should have tried again. But we—I—knew you would not do that. So many predicaments has your stupidity placed you in, and always you react in the same manner. You place no faith in the wisdom or mercy of constituted authority. You make no study of the factors behind your contretemps. Tricks you have, not brains; tricks and legs. So, where tricks are futile, you run."

Toddy grunted. "You're a funny guy, Milt. Very funny."

"Oh, there is no doubt about it. Everyone has always said so. There is only one person who did not."

"Me," cooed Elaine, snuggling against him. "I knew better right from the beginning."

"So you did," Milt nodded benignly. "So now, I think, you should have another drink. A very small one."

Ahead and to the right, blurred lights pushed up through the shrouds of rain. Santa Monica. It wouldn't be long now.

A car came towards them, fog-lights burning, moving rapidly. Toddy's hand tightened on the wheel . . . Sideswipe it? . . . Huh-uh. Milt had nothing to lose. An accident, any sign of trouble, would only make him kill more quickly.

Toddy forced a short ugly laugh. Elaine lowered the bottle, squinted suspiciously in the darkness.

"Something funny, prince?"

Toddy shrugged.

"Goddammit, I asked you if—"

"Quiet, my treasure." Milt drew her back against his

shoulder. "And, yes, I think I will take charge of the liquor. He is trying to disturb you. Drink makes the task easy."

"But—all right, honey."

"There's one thing I don't understand," said Toddy. "Why was the room straightened up before Elaine skipped out?"

"On the night of her supposed death? Merely a precautionary measure. The police might have been notified if the condition of the room happened to be observed. I felt sure you would hold Alvarado responsible. I wished to make sure you had no interference."

"That part of your plan didn't work out very well, did it?"

"It worked out well enough," said Milt, "as your present situation proves. . . . But you were laughing a moment ago?"

"I was just thinking." Toddy laughed again. "Wondering about you and Elaine; how long it'll be before she turns on you . . . when you least expect it."

"Because she turned, as you put it, on you? But there is no similarity between the two cases. You could give her nothing. I can. She never needed you. She needs me. You tried to hold her against her will. I would never do that. If parting becomes necessary, it will be arranged amicably. We will share and share alike, and each will go his own way."

"That's sound logic," said Toddy, "but you're not dealing with a logical person. Elaine gets her fun out of not getting along. It's the only entertainment, aside from drinking, that she's capable of. She's a degenerate, Milt. She's liable to go in for killing as hard as she does drinking. I wouldn't believe the doctors when—"

Something hit him a painful blow on the head, the car

swerved. He swung it straight again at a sharp command from Milt. In the rear-view mirror, he saw the jeweler turn, hand raised, toward Elaine.

"*Dummkopf!*" he snapped. "I have a notion to . . ." Then he smiled, and his voice went suddenly gentle. "It seems we both have the temper. It is not a time to give way to it."

"I'm sorry, honey. He just made me so damned sore . . ."

"But now you see through his tricks, eh? You see where they might lead to?"

"Uh-huh." Elaine sighed. "You're so smart, darling. You see right through people."

"He doesn't see through you," said Toddy. "If he did he'd take that gun away from you. He'd know what you're thinking—that all of that dough would be better than half."

Elaine made a mocking sound with her lips. Milt chuckled fatly.

"It is useless, Toddy. In the regrettable absence of attraction, there would still be the factor of need. It was I who planned this, and there will be yet more planning, thinking, to be done. Even an Elaine as elemental as the one you portray would not destroy something necessary to survival."

"Anyway," said Elaine, "I don't want the old gun; I wouldn't know how to use it. You take it, honey."

Milt pushed it back at her. "But you must know! It is imperative. Look, I will show you again . . . The safety, here. Then, only a firm, short pull on the trigger. Very short unless you wish to empty it. It is automatic, as I told you previously . . ."

His own gun was in his lap for the moment, and Toddy

knew another surge of hope. He couldn't, of course, do anything himself. But Elaine . . .

But Elaine didn't. Milt picked up his gun again.

Toddy turned the car off Olympic and onto Ocean Avenue. They reached Pico Street, and he turned again. Less than a mile ahead was the ocean.

"No more questions, Toddy? Nothing else you would like to inquire about?"

"Nothing."

"After all, the opportunity will not arise again."

"No, it won't," said Toddy. "Look, Milt . . ."

"Yes?"

"Let Miss Chavez go. She won't—"

"I will not go," said Dolores, calmly.

"You will not," agreed Milt. "I am sorry. It is a terrible penalty to pay for allying oneself with an imbecile."

He rolled down the window of the car and peered out, and the rain sounds mingled with the roar of the ocean, the breakers rolling in and out from shore. Toddy made the last turn.

"You made one mistake, Milt. There's one thing you didn't count on."

"Interesting," murmured Milt, "but not, I am afraid, true. . . . This is the place you had in mind, I believe? Yes. You will stop, then, and turn off your lights."

Toddy stopped. The lights went off.

There was a moment of silence, the near-absolute silence which precedes action. Before Milt could break it, Toddy spoke.

This was his last chance, his and Dolores'. And he knew it was wasted, no chance at all, even before he started to speak. What he had to say was incredible. His strained, hollow voice made it preposterous.

"Really, Toddy." Milt sounded almost embarrassed. "You do not expect us to believe that?"

"No," said Toddy. "I don't expect you to believe me. But it is true."

"Only stupidity I charged you with," Milt pointed out. "Not insanity. You did not know Elaine was alive. You were sure you would be accused of her murder. Willing though you might be to pass up a fortune, and I sincerely suspect such a willingness, you would not dare abide by your bargain. In this case, you had no choice but to run."

"I was tired of running." (*Elaine giggled.*) "I knew I hadn't killed her. I was going to fight the case."

"Without money? With all the evidence against you? With a long record of criminality? And if, by some fluke of justice, you cleared yourself, what then? You have no trade but to prey upon others. You—"

"I could get one." The words, the tone seemed ridiculously childish.

"We waste time," said Milt. "You would have me believe you pursued one futility to achieve another. You, risking your liberty—perhaps your life—by keeping a bargain? You, placing your faith, at last, in the courts? You, Toddy Kent, doing these things for a so-called good name, a job, perhaps Miss Chavez—"

"It would not have been perhaps," said Dolores.

"Even so," Milt shrugged. "I know him too well, and he knows himself too well. He does not fit the part. . . . Now, I think . . ."

"Let Elaine think," Toddy persisted doggedly. "You can't pull out. You want to get her in as deep as you are. Don't let him do it, Elaine! There's a tape recorder in the car. I—"

"Elaine," Milt interrupted, "is not required to think. And, of course, there is a recorder. How else could you obtain the evidence you were supposed to get? I do not deny the existence of a bargain. Only that you had no intention of keeping it."

"I did intend to keep it! I know it looks like I didn't, but I had to make it look that way! I was supposed to meet them here—I called them just before I went to your shop. Elaine—"

"Tonight?" said Milt. "You were to meet them there tonight, or tomorrow night? Or perhaps even the next? You are transparent, Toddy. Your government men would have given you two days without surveillance as quickly as they would give you two hours. Never would they have agreed to such an arrangement."

"They didn't agree to it, but they had to take it. I'd already ducked out on 'em. It was either play it my way or—"

"Nonsense. You insult my intelligence."

"Now, wait a minute," said Elaine, worriedly. "Let me—"

"It is not necessary," said Milt. "I have already thought. Of everything . . . You were to meet them here, eh? Bah! Where are they, then?"

Toddy licked dry lips, helplessly. It was no use. The evidence was all against him. He couldn't make them believe something that was incredible to himself.

"I don't know," he said, almost indifferently. "It's a big beach. Maybe they don't recognize the car. I don't know where they are, but—"

Milt's curt, bored laugh cut him off. "They would not recognize the car, certainly. You would see to that. And we both know where they are—anywhere but here. Now, enough!"

"But Milt, honey . . ." Elaine began.

"Enough!" snapped Milt. "Must I explain everything twice? Why do you think I played with him there in the

shop, found out exactly where he wished to go? Because it
would be safe. It would be the last place his whilom
friends would expect to find him."

"All right, honey. I was just—"

"We will proceed! And—*please!*—the bottle will remain
here!"

Dolores was shoved over in the seat, squeezed against
Toddy. Elaine pushed past her, and got out. She stood back
in the sand a few feet, covering the door as Toddy and the
girl emerged.

Milt came out last, grunting from the exertion, blinking
his eyes against the rain.

"Now," he panted, "we will just . . ." He gestured with
the gun. Elaine spoke apologetically.

"Milt, baby, are you sure, really sure that . . . ?"

"I have said so! It is all finished. Now we have only to—"

He saw, then, heard the childishly delighted laugh—
mischievous, filled with the viciousness it could not recognize, signaling triumph in a game without rules. It seemed
to paralyze him. The gun hung loose in his fingers.

"*Liebling!*" he gasped. "Darling! There is so much.
Why—?"

There was a brief, stuttering blast. "W-why?" Milt said,
and crumpled to the sand. And he said no more and heard
no more.

Elaine snatched up his gun, and leveled it quickly.

"Huh-uh, prince. You gave me an idea, but I get ideas,
too. L'il Elaine's dead. L'il Elaine's in the clear. This is your
gun and you shot him, and he shot you and her. And—"

"Elaine!" Toddy's voice shook. "For your own sake,
don't! The government men are bound to be near here.
They probably missed us in the rain, but those shots are
sure to—"

"D—don't make me laugh, prince. D-don't m-make me laugh . . ."

She began to rock with laughter; it pealed out, shrill, delighted, infectious. And suddenly Toddy was laughing with her. Laughing and ridding himself of something, the last, fragile, frazzled tie. "L-like"—she was shrieking—"like Milt said, prince, you d-don't fit the part!"

That was the way he would always remember her—the monkey face twisted with merriment, the scrawny, rain-drenched figure rocking in the abrupt pitiless glow of floodlights, laughing as the guns of the T-men began to chatter.

So he would always remember her, but it was like remembering another person. Someone he had never known.

The gizmo, the golden, deceptive, brass-filled gizmo, was gone at last.

THE END

ALSO AVAILABLE FROM JIM THOMPSON

> "Jim Thompson is the best suspense writer going, bar none."
> —*The New York Times*

AFTER DARK, MY SWEET

William Collins is very handsome, very polite, and very dangerous when aroused. Now Collins, a onetime boxer, has broken out of his fourth mental institution and met up with an affable con man and a highly arousing woman, whose plans for him include kidnapping, murder, and more.

Fiction/Crime/0-679-73247-0

THE GRIFTERS

Roy Dillon, the con man. Lily Dillon, his mother. Moira Langtry, his mistress. Carol Roberg, his nurse—the victim. Together these four make up a quadrangle of greed and perverse love in Jim Thompson's mesmerizing novel of corruption.

Fiction/Crime/0-679-73248-9

THE KILLER INSIDE ME

Lou Ford is the deputy sheriff of a small town in Texas. The worst thing most people can say against him is that he's a little slow and a little boring. But, then, most people don't know about the sickness—the sickness that almost got Lou put away when he was younger. The sickness that is about to surface again.

Fiction/Crime/0-679-73397-3

POP. 1280

Pop. 1280 is a chilling and brutally funny romp through the id of the American South, and the basis for an acclaimed French *film noir*, *Coup de Torchon*.

Fiction/Crime/0-679-73249-7